Alistair Mackay

The Lucky Ones
and other stories

Kwela Books

Cover design by Marius Roux

Originally printed in South Africa
ISBN: 978-0-7957-1016-2 (First edition, first impression 2025)

LSiPOD: 978-0-7957-1119-0 (First edition, first impression 2025)

ISBN 978-0-7957-1019-3 (epub)

Praise for Alistair Mackay's writing:

'An important, if not essential, voice of contemporary South Africa.'
– CA Davids

'Fresh, unflinching and propulsive.' – SJ Naudé

'Revolutionary. Vulnerable. Chilling in its relevance.'
– Mia Arderne

'It's brutal and heartbreaking and undoubtedly brilliant.'
– Sanet Oberholzer, *Sunday Times*

'*It Doesn't Have to Be This Way* is an exquisitely crafted story of love
and loss, identity and humanity, as Mackay weaves together the
complexity of being a human in the world today.'
– Sarah Hoek, *Daily Maverick*

'Brimming with talent.' – Deborah Steinmair, V*ryeweekblad*

'*The Child* is a remarkable achievement, showcasing Mackay's
talent for crafting deeply affecting narratives that resonate
with readers on a profound level. It is a testament to the
power of storytelling.'
– Shaun Lunga, *Sunday Times*

'One of South Africa's most promising young writers.'
– Jean Meiring, *Die Burger*

'Outrageously beautiful . . . *The Child* is healing literature.'
– Siya Khumalo, *News24*

Contents

Fever Tree

Jeremy slammed the car door. Ignition off, windows up. His skin came alive in a thousand tiny pinpricks and soon he was coated in a thin film of sweat. His body felt lighter in the heat, less constricted. His hands stopped shaking. His mind went blank.

He waited like this for some time. How long, he didn't know. He watched a young man in seemingly good health weave slowly between the parked cars and enter the hospital. He watched a mother and daughter come out a few minutes later, the mother in sunglasses, the daughter transfixed by her phone. On a nearby car hazard lights flashed twice. The women got in, the mother starting the engine. They looked right through him as their sedan turned and drove out. He was invisible in his hatchback with its dented bumper and its 'anti-hijack' windows, a feature David thought was a good idea when Jeremy bought the car, though how a membrane of darkness on the glass could protect him from anything is anyone's guess.

There's nothing wrong with your heart, the doctor had said. You see here on the chart, it's well within normal range.

What other tests can we do?

We don't need to. Your heart is fine.

I can feel the pain right now. It's happening right now.

Have you been taking the pills I prescribed?

Jeremy went to the pharmacy on his way out, just in case the doctor could tell he'd never filled the script. The pills were torpedo shaped with a groove in the middle to facilitate breaking them in half. They were exactly the wrong shade of blue, the one with all the connotations he didn't like: nurses' uniforms, hospital corridors, the sky in some mind-control dystopia where everything is a little off. Greyed out by drugs he didn't need, for an anxiety disorder he didn't have. If he were anxious, he would know. He wouldn't need chest pains to tell him.

He turned on his phone and placed it in the cup compartment between the seats. Who could he even tell about this most recent trip to the hospital? His mother didn't know about these visits. He'd stopped telling his friends when they became a weekly thing. And David, of course. The only person he really wanted to talk to about any of this was David.

I'm okay, he said to the empty car around him.

I'm okay.

It's just a minor infection, he said to his boss when he got back to the office. Should clear up in a few days. He sat down at his desk. She continued to stand there, smiling at him like she didn't believe he'd been to the doctor at all. All warmth and glittering pity in the eyes. You know we understand if you need a bit more time, she said. Why don't you take the afternoon off?

Thanks, he said. I'm fine. She squeezed his shoulder. He got up to go to the kitchenette, mostly so he didn't have to look at the excruciating kindness in her face. She didn't follow him. She let him go.

He made himself a large mug of Earl Grey tea even though it's caffeinated and the doctor told him to go easy on caffeine for a while. He opened the document he'd been working on before leaving for the hospital. A listicle of ten things not to miss if you have forty-eight hours in New York City. Jeremy had never been to New York, but it didn't matter. Plenty of other people had been and so the job was really just researching and repackaging the content. Finding the right influencers to quote. Make it quirky and memorable and fun, his boss had said. He'd wanted to say, New York is a sixteen-hour flight away. If our readers go, they'll stay longer than a weekend. But he didn't. He said, I'll have it with you by the end of today.

Kyle came over. He clicked his fingers in Jeremy's face.

I said hi, Jeremy!

Oh. Hey.

A little zoned out there, are we?

Jeremy realised he hadn't been looking at his screen. He'd been staring at the small fever tree on his desk, the one David gave him on his first day at this job. They're magical, David had said, they photosynthesise with their bark. That's why they're green. Do you know how few trees do that? Early Europeans thought that just being near them made you sick. It was probably malaria, but they thought the trees made you see things. Inyangas use their bark to make people lucid dream.

Jeremy's tree didn't look powerful enough to do any of that. It looked delicate and forlorn, far from sun-kissed savannahs and lazy rivers and nibbling giraffes. Its leaves had gone yellow and Jeremy wished he knew how to fix that. He could almost feel the desperation with which its tiny roots clung to the soil, searching for stability in a tray that could be knocked off the desk without even trying, its whole world shattered on the floor by mistake. He'd told David he loved bonsais, but it wasn't right to do this to another living thing. It wasn't fair.

He scrunched up his face and said, Urgh, I'm struggling with this listicle.

Listen, a few of us are going for drinks after work. I think you should come.

I have yoga tonight.

Can't you miss it this once? Kyle tilted his head and pouted his lips in a gesture that seemed kind of flirty and it made the pain flare in Jeremy's chest. He stood up to put a bit of distance between himself and Kyle. He felt dizzy. The dizziness had come and gone for a few days now, swooping in without warning. It made the lights too bright and the details on faces impossible to see. Everything was too close and too far away at the same time, and the nauseous disorientation wasn't even the worst thing about it. The worst thing was that he was losing his mind, falling backwards into madness or developing some debilitating mental disability like early onset Alzheimer's that would trap him forever in a terrifying, confusing senselessness. He would go back to the hospital tomorrow but to a different doctor this time, someone who listened to what he said instead of implying he was insane. He wasn't imagining the things he felt. He wasn't inventing ailments out of boredom. Even hypochondriacs get sick and die, he'd said to his doctor recently, half in jest but half to make the point that he wanted the examination to be thorough. No one's calling you a hypochondriac, his doctor had said, wounded and, suddenly, patronisingly gentle, but he still hadn't given Jeremy the test he wanted.

Sorry, no. Yoga really helps me.

Kyle straightened his neck and nodded. Of course, he said. Join us afterwards?

He didn't ask: helps with what? The buzz Jeremy felt at having admitted something real and vulnerable to another human being dissipated into the electric glow of the open-plan office.

He sent off his listicle, dropped his mug into the sink and returned to his desk to water his bonsai slowly with teaspoons of water until the hard silver surface of the soil softened and darkened and became porous. He was in the yoga studio by 17:15, stretching his hamstrings on his gun-metal-grey mat. The class didn't start until 17:30 but he liked to get there early, find a spot before the others arrived in a frenzied wave at 17:28. They tiptoed into the studio in silence, cringed when they asked people to move up, tried to squeeze in between those who were already meditating on their mats. Jeremy hated it. Just watching them do this made him feel tense. The clownish, overacted displays of apology. The repressed irritation.

He tried to ignore everyone in the room. He watched the hundreds of tiny, multicoloured origami butterflies that fluttered on the front wall and ceiling of the studio. They looked ready to take flight in the breeze that blew in through the windows, alive almost, in the golden evening light – but of course they weren't alive. They were just paper. Long dead trees, mulched, bleached, dyed, cut.

Yoga had been his therapist's idea and even though he stopped going to see her because he had nothing left to say, her advice on this had been right. It did help. He focused on his breathing, became conscious of the expansion of his lungs and his chest. He moved slowly through the class, bending backwards and twisting his torso and holding the positions with the muscles of his core, hidden now by a little pillow of fat that hadn't been there a few months ago. He let the instructor correct his posture a few times and he held back the tears when she touched him, when she pressed her warm hands on his lower back or gently squeezed his shoulder in encouragement and the urge to sob almost overwhelmed him. He surrendered to it at the end of the class, when the instructor turned off the lights and put on soothing music for the period of meditation. It was dark by then and no one could see him. He closed his eyes and allowed the tears to come streaming out in silence. He liked to imagine he was a tree, and the fluid leaking from his eyes was clear, sweet sap pouring from a gash in his bark. This image made it feel less desperate. It wasn't sadness he felt, anyway. It wasn't anything. A mechanical process of the body, a muscular release. But it must be good for him; for the briefest moment afterwards, there was no dread. No heaviness in his gut.

The instructor suggested they start to wiggle their fingers and toes, to return their attention to the room. Jeremy used this time to pull himself together, as his father used to say. Finding a deep reserve of strength within himself, he crushed any lingering impulse to cry, hardened his insides, and wiped his eyes. His face was dry just in time for the lights to come back on.

Namaste, said the instructor.

Namaste, they all replied, bowing back.

He turned on his phone on his way out. Three messages from Kyle. He would ignore them until later that night when it was too late to join him. Sorry, only saw these now, he'd say. Next time.

On the short walk from the yoga studio to his car he stepped past two fallen galaxies of glass on the pavement. Shattered car windows. He was approached by a beggar with the obsequious manner of someone about to mug him. The beggar followed him, getting closer with every increasingly rapid step Jeremy took. The beggar started to say something else when Jeremy fumbled for his car keys, perhaps abandoning his story of hunger and shoelessness for threats and abuse – Jeremy couldn't tell, his heart was thundering in his ears – and only when a large man came out of a nearby house with a pit bull on a leash did the beggar move away. Jeremy's hands were shaking as he locked the car door. He started the engine. He did not want to be alone in his flat. Not before the landlord installed alarm sensors on the balcony like he'd asked.

He typed a message to Kyle while waiting at a traffic light.

You guys still out?

Come and join us!

Jeremy left his car at home and took an Uber because he knew he'd need to drink. He hated the idea of spending an evening with virtual strangers. Aside from Kyle, he'd met Jason once before but the others were new – Alex, S'bu and a slightly older guy called Anthony. Jeremy tried his hardest to be gregarious and witty but all he could really think about was how terrible it was that he was afraid of people on the street. How does a society ever get over that? Kyle made a joke and Jeremy forced a laugh out of his throat but it sounded more like a bark, and what was the point? All of them could tell he was a fake.

He decided to forego a second beer and get a martini instead. It was a dramatic thing to order (maybe normal if you lived in New York? Or in a movie?) but it was the only way to get the necessary level of alcohol into his system in a reasonable amount of time. What he really wanted to drink was six shots of whiskey, but no bar had invented a name for a drink like that and it wouldn't be served in a fancy triangular glass that disguised his dependence.

Their voices were disappearing. Alex, Anthony. Fading away just as Jeremy expected. It happened every time he tried to socialise. Soon, instead of hearing the words they said, he'd hear only their malicious intentions, the things they thought, that they said with their eyes but would never say out loud. He could hear it all. The same soundtrack as in his childhood, over and over on a loop but this time with different voices. You're boring. You're too quiet. Nobody likes you. Why do we invite you to things?

They had invited him to this. He needed to prove he was worth it.

He widened his eyes. Lifted the muscles in his cheeks. Impersonated the charming, extroverted people he saw on Netflix. How do you know Kyle? he said to S'bu.

Through Twitter.

This struck Jeremy as unbearably sad, though he wasn't sure why. He didn't know how to continue the conversation after that. Is Kyle funny on Twitter? he should say. Or: what do you guys write about? All of it sounded so stupid before it left his mouth. He stared at his drink. Another successful attempt to socialise.

I like the James Bond thing, S'bu said.

What?

The martini. It's very James Bond.

Oh! Right.

It's just a joke, man.

I know. I get it. It's just, I think martinis have been around longer than James Bond.

S'bu raised his eyebrows. Jeremy took a large sip and stifled the shudder that electrified his spine. He absorbed the movement back into his body.

Do you work with Kyle?

The room was loud. S'bu was very close to his ear. It was awkward to make eye contact so Jeremy turned his gaze to the chequerboard floor tiles.

Sort of, Jeremy said. He's in styling and I'm a copywriter, but yeah, same office.

Cool.

What do you do?

Jeremy missed S'bu's answer because Kyle declared that it was time to dance.

Jesus! It's a school night, said Alex. But Kyle rolled his eyes and waved the comment away.

And so? Are we octogenarians?

Jeremy hated the way Kyle used 'octogenarians' to denote anything boring and old-fashioned. The first time he'd said it had been to refer to Jeremy's monogamous relationship with David, but he used it for all kinds of behaviour he disliked. Sleeping the recommended eight hours. Reading books. Caring about the people around you. As if old people weren't more impressive than all of them put together. Any actual octogenarians had survived things Jeremy couldn't bear, the maladies lurking around every corner. Brain tumours and colon cancer and auto-immune diseases and road deaths and hijackings and stabbings on the street and terrorism and drought. They had lost their looks. Lost many of the people they loved. They had been through more than Kyle could imagine and Kyle used them as a punchline. He was so smug when he said it, too, as if dressing up his judgement in a Latin-sounding, multisyllabic word made him sophisticated and cuttingly witty, rather than petty and mean. Jeremy hated that Kyle had a favourite word at all. How lazy and emotionally stunted it was to view all of life's nuance and complexity through the binary of old and boring versus young and cool. It made Jeremy feel trapped in a life that was far too small for him. And surrounded by small, narrow-minded people.

No, Kyle answered himself, we're young and we can do whatever the hell we want. He stood up and gestured at Jeremy to follow him into the dance space. Jeremy finished his drink and ordered another.

Jeremy reached for S'bu's forearm. You should dance too, he said. He was relieved to discover that he was slurring his speech. Syllables pitched and rolled, knocked into each other like waves in a storm. They'd soon drown the cacophony inside his head.

S'bu looked amused to be included in whatever was going on between Jeremy and Kyle but he got up from the table and danced along. Narrowing his eyes, Kyle glared at him. S'bu lifted his hands as if to say, don't shoot.

You like this place? S'bu asked.

Jeremy lurched to the side. It's ordinary, he said.

I suppose so, S'bu said. That's not so bad, is it?

Jeremy put his hand on S'bu's neck and spoke far too close to his ear. I don't know. I think ordinary is kind of horrifying, you know? Can't we be *extra*-ordinary? He paused for a moment to marvel at how well he had said the word, separating the parts to reveal its history, a meaning he thought was lost, a meaning that was suddenly, movingly profound.

Like, if every moment isn't important, what are we doing?

He felt an expulsion of air against his cheek. A short, sharp laugh.

We're having a good time? S'bu said.

I write a load of crap for a living, Jeremy continued. I spend my life sitting at a desk writing about things I've never done. Life is so short and we have so little time and there are people travelling across Asia living in caravans and people becoming famous musicians or teaching rural kids how to read and I'm here, doing whatever this is. He gestured to the room around them.

Sure, S'bu said.

Don't you think we'll regret so much of this when we're dying?

S'bu turned down the sides of his mouth to look earnest. I kinda like my job, he said.

Jeremy let go of S'bu's neck and spun away from him in something like a dance move. He couldn't look at anything in the bar. The drunken faces of the patrons, weathered and false, laughing uproariously at things that weren't funny, the dated decor with scuffed edges, the tiles that needed scrubbing. Ordinary. All of it was so ordinary and depressing and the clock was ticking for each of them. Was this all they were ever going to get?

Ignore him, he heard Kyle say softly to S'bu when he thought the music would drown out his voice. His partner just died.

Jeremy spun back towards the two of them and he took S'bu's face in his hands and kissed him. Right there in front of all the straight people in the bar. In front of Kyle. Warm, wet tongue. Breath of cigarettes and beer.

Kyle recoiled and turned towards the booth but Jeremy grabbed his hand and pulled Kyle towards him and kissed him in the same messy way.

Let's go back to my place.

Jeremy was aware, even while it was happening, that the evening had the quality of a memory. Hazy and warm, fading in and out of focus. He could speak freely about what he wanted. For once, he knew what that was. He wanted to be fucked by S'bu as he made out with Kyle. He wanted to be tied up and used by both of them without being able to see who was doing it. The two of them acquiesced. They flipped him over and moved him around like he was weightless, like he wasn't even there. Their eyes sparkled black with shame and lust and something else.

Golden light from his desk lamp. By some alchemy of its glow and of semiconsciousness he could hear himself speaking, hear the words falling from his mouth and they matched what he was saying inside. A perfect logic of thought into word, word into action. A parallel universe without waste, without loss. No entropy and no misunderstanding. Jeremy watched their blurry torsos in the small gap between his lower eyelid and the necktie wrapped around his head. He breathed in the smell of deodorised sweat.

He fell asleep between them in the end. Held tight by their solid, breathing bodies. A vice in which he could not move. Didn't want to move.

He woke with his head on Kyle's chest. A crack of blue light between the curtains. He thought: this is not the position I'd have expected to wake up in with Kyle. He should be sleeping on my chest. He's smaller than me. I should be the protector.

His thoughts were interrupted by the sound of Kyle's heartbeat, soft and steady against Jeremy's ear. A quiet thumping. Heartbeats: so fragile and beautiful and almost always unnoticed. Kyle's heart was working to keep Kyle alive, straining and pumping and pushing and unable ever to take a break. No rest and no thanks and no room to fuck up. Jeremy felt his own heart beating in his chest as he lay there. Unobtrusive and small.

So I guess I'll see you, S'bu said. He was sitting at the foot of the bed, fully dressed, tying the laces of his shoes. That was a weird night, but thanks.

Not so octogenarian, was it?

What?

You don't want to stay for coffee? Jeremy said.

Dude, are you okay?

Jeremy felt his cheek. He looked down at the wet patch on Kyle's chest.

Do you want to talk about it?

What was the point of talking about it? Would talking bring David back? Would talking ensure Kyle's heart kept beating? Jeremy's therapist had wanted to talk about it too, as if Jeremy's sadness could be fixed, as if sadness wasn't the background feeling of the whole fucking world, of being alive, of losing everything as you tried to hold on to it. The end was rushing towards each of them and there was nothing they could do to prepare, to delay. He'd watched David fight with all of his strength and waste away regardless,

21

becoming smaller every week, less coherent, less himself. He'd watched David's terrified eyes right to the end. No final moment of peaceful acceptance. No answers to what any of it means. What if it means nothing? Consciousness as an evolutionary mistake. Something we have and then we don't. Does talking make that easier to accept?

It's nothing, Jeremy said, sometimes hangovers make me weepy is all. Thanks, though.

I'm not going to stay for coffee, if that's okay.

Of course. Thanks again.

He left the flat before Kyle woke up and called in sick to work. He assumed Kyle would do the same.

At the park, Jeremy unpacked his book and his kikoi and a bottle of water. He unfolded the kikoi beneath a large fever tree and lay down on his back to watch the branches tickle the sky. This tree was happier than the one back at the office. Its leaves were full and green, its roots deep in the earth, its thorny branches stretched out beyond reach. Trees are meant to be like this, he thought. Comforting in their size and stability and relative permanence. Ancient and spiritual, if there is such a thing.

A hot wind came up and shook the branches above him and blew some grit into his eyes, and he knew that it was a precursor of worse things. Heatwaves and droughts and hurricanes. Whole ecosystems were collapsing already. There were fewer birds in this park than he remembered, he was sure of it, fewer than when he started coming here. Forests were disappearing across the globe while politicians called it pseudoscience, a Chinese hoax. Trees are no match for us. Even the ancient, sturdy ones, even the ones we haven't trapped in tiny bonsai dishes, they can't survive us. They can't survive our clearings and our emissions. We'll burn the planet to the ground for bigger houses, faster cars, faster AI, ideologies that don't work.

The pain was starting in his chest again. He took a few deep breaths, tried to count to five on each inhalation. He opened his book to distract himself, but he'd lost the ability to read. His eyes moved back and forth over the lines but the words had no meaning. They were shapes in ink, symbols from some forgotten civilisation. The ideas were trapped behind the paper, inaccessible. The symbols blurred in his eyes. Pain shot from his chest to his abdomen. Whatever was wrong with him was spreading. He was near enough to the hospital that he could run to the Emergency Room before he collapsed, but would it be better to run so the doctors had more time or to walk slowly so as not to exacerbate the strain on his heart?

He heard voices near the fountain. He was certain one of them belonged to his boss. She would see that he'd been lying about being sick today. He'd been lying about being sick yesterday, too. He didn't look sick. He never looked as sick as he felt.

He took a sip of water and tried to talk himself out of it.

If the pain is sharp it's not cardiovascular, his doctor had said. This pain was sharp. Like a knife between the ribs.

He stuffed his belongings into his bag and moved away from the hospital side of the park, away from the fountain and down towards the bottom corner. Here, beside the public toilets, homeless people had built an oasis away from the real world. The trees sparkled in silver and blue, their trunks and branches wrapped in tinsel. Gold and silver orbs trembled beneath their leaves. There were paper mache sculptures of Pegasus and Pan. There were beautiful arrangements of flowers – fresh, dead and drying – stuffed into painted rubber tyres and hollowed-out tree trunks. Rainwater was diverted from the paved gutters into hand-dug channels in the soil flanked by arum lilies and birds-of-paradise, a network of tiny streams and opulent gardens. There were chessboards and cardboard boxes and shopping trolleys full of junk. Homeless people lay asleep on sleeping bags, sat on logs, fed the pigeons. Stray dogs guarded their little kingdom, but they sniffed Jeremy's legs and decided to let him pass.

Do you mind if I sit here? he said to the woman sitting closest to him. She looked him up and down and waved towards the grass. Please, she said.

Guilt constricted around his heart. The way he'd run from the beggar on the street. The way he closed his car windows whenever he pulled up to an intersection where people were asking for money.

You're very kind, he said. He spread his kikoi in a small clearing on the lawn. He looked behind him to see if his boss had followed but there was no one coming for him. Nothing but trees. The woman caught his eye and smiled. She looked tired.

Jeremy lay down on his back and closed his eyes. He imagined roots growing from his fingertips and his toes. Extending out of his flesh and down into the earth, burrowing deeper and deeper, anchoring him to this place, this time. Steady and solid and safe, even in the wind. I'm okay, he said to himself. I'm okay.

What? the woman said.

He smiled with the sunshine on his eyelids. Nothing. I was talking to myself.

Oh, she said, you're one of those.

Maybe he was one of those. Maybe he should stop trying to fight it. He opened his eyes and fumbled in his bag for the pills he'd never wanted. They were the same sickening blue as yesterday. Grey and murky and unnatural, but maybe he needed something unnatural. Maybe we'd stripped nature of its power to heal us. Both of us on life support, he said to the trees. He cracked open the plastic tube and tipped a torpedo into his palm. The trees spun around him, green and silver catching the light, but the spinning wasn't real. He wasn't sick. He had to try to remember that. How do you remember what you've never believed?

Can I have one? the homeless woman asked.

It's not a painkiller, he said.

It doesn't matter.

He gave her a tablet and swallowed his down dry. She came and sat next to him on his kikoi. Her smell was earthy and rich. She took his hand in hers.

Oh, he said. No. I'm gay.

She looked at him and laughed. Relax, she said, but she didn't let go of his hand. How easy it would be to stay here. Never to go back to his repetitive, terrifying life. Offices and small talk and descent and disease. Is this what happened to some people? They checked out. Wound up living in parks and begging at the traffic lights because they couldn't bear it.

He looked up at the sky.

I don't want the colour to go, he said.

Okay, she laughed. I don't know what nonsense you're talking, but that's okay.

Young People Problems

In spite of everything, the heat is relentless. I move slowly so I don't lose too much sweat. I may be walking for hours and dehydration is inevitable, but too much exertion and I won't survive the morning. There's no wind today. No wind for the first time in weeks. I can take the parasol with me. I can shade my face from the falling fire.

The rocky mountainside beside me dances in the heat. Gravel and dust in ochres and browns, dead trees and bushes in black. The bleached grey tar is the same as it was in my childhood. I imagine the mountains as they were, then. Greens and golds and pinks. Fynbos stretched right up into the rocky crags. Bright clumps of geometric protea flowers. Intricate silver leaves. Seasonal streams chattered over the rocks and baboons barked their warning to the echoes. There were birds overhead. Lizards and dassies and hikers.

There are still lizards, I think. And snakes, though who knows what the snakes eat. Other snakes, I suppose. We have pumped out a Mesozoic atmosphere, unfit for mammals with heat trapped in our blood.

We have returned the world to the reptiles.

I must drive the bus to the city this afternoon, to fetch a child. And so now I must find enough people to fill it. The rules against single-occupancy vehicles are strict, or perhaps I impose a stricter rule on myself because I find the carbon calculations impossibly complicated. Engine efficiency, distance travelled, number of passengers, weight. Add to that the hidden ways in which we contribute to the carbon emissions in a year – how many late nights did I spend reading in bed with the light on? – and all of it just gets to be too much. Too many variables. Severe punishment for overshooting the annual allowance. Rather play it safe. The more passengers in the bus, the better.

In some countries, I believe, motorised travel is barely restricted, because the vehicles are electric and the grid is powered by wind and sun. But our grid still relied on fossil fuels when the Day of Judgement came, and so the whole system was shut down. We run on solar power now, in our village, but I think our bus burns a single person's yearly carbon quota in two trips to the city. There will be young people keeping track.

Besides the orphanage, there are about a hundred homes in our village, scattered in dusty, barren yards as if dropped haphazardly from the sky. I stop at the first house – a squat, yellow bungalow with shuttered windows and an open front door. I knock on the metal doorframe. A young man emerges from the dark interior. Shirtless, sweaty. His lean muscles glisten. The fabric of his blue shorts is damp where it meets his skin.

'Good morning, sir,' I say. I lower my eyes. 'I came to ask if anyone here would like a lift to the city.'

He looks me up and down. He takes a bite of a crisp, green apple. Juice runs over his lightly stubbled chin. Where did he find an apple? He wipes his mouth, then his forehead. 'Maybe. Let me know once you have ten others,' he says.

'I will do, sir. And how many will be coming from this house if you do decide to join us?'

He tilts his head back. Looks down his nose at me. 'I am alone,' he says. 'There are no pathogens here.'

I feel my cheeks flush, though I wish they wouldn't. I'm only thirty-four, only four years too old to be allowed in leadership. Do I look older than that? I'm not a pathogen, I want to explain, but he hasn't directly accused me of anything, and what do I call myself, anyway? They haven't bothered coming up with a name for my generation. The Ones Who Knew What Was Coming And Didn't Do Anything To Stop It?

'Right, sir, so just the one, then.'

There's a smirk on his face now. He's enjoying his power.

'Do you want to know what happened to them?' he says. It's rhetorical, of course. I can't disrespect my youngers. I want to know whatever he wants to tell me.

'Of course, sir.'

'Burned alive,' he says. Smiling, satisfied.

My mouth is dry. I never get used to this. I wish I could lick the droplet of apple juice he missed on his chin. I wish he would offer me some water. I wish I could stand beneath a cold shower and never leave it. Let it soak and cool my skin. Maybe I'd open my mouth and let the water pour in, fill me up and drown me. Burning alive is one of the worst sentences. Prescribed for only the most heinous offenders. His parents must have worked for an oil company or—

'They were coal miners,' he says, and I think I might be sick. These measures were put in place to stop the powerful. Mine owners, big business lobbyists, boards of the energy companies – fine, but don't burn the lowly mineworkers.

'I'm sorry for your loss,' I say.

He narrows his eyes at me. 'You're dismissed.'

The second home I try is smaller than the first. Sky blue with peeling paint and a large section of roof missing. The dry yard is divided into squares, each square sectioned into rows of ridges. A few poles are left standing in the dirt, perhaps from a time when they supported tomatoes or grapevines. A trellis arch above the front door, webbed together by twisting dead wood. An elderly woman stands in the doorway. Her face is lined, soft with kindness, the same ochre colour as the sand and rock outside. 'Come in,' she says, and she takes me to her little living room. A threadbare armchair. A lumpy, olive green couch. She tremors a little as she moves, but she is lithe, energetic.

'It's lovely to see an old person,' I say, as she hands me a glass of lukewarm water. I don't need to say, you never see old people any more.

She winks at me. 'I escaped the retribution,' she tells me, 'because I'm untainted.'

'I didn't know we had untainted in our village,' I say, laughing because she must be joking. 'We're so close to the city!' There were no untainted in this country, were there? Further north, in the jungles of Central Africa, maybe. And of course on remote islands and the Arctic. There, an indigenous way of life could survive. A reverence for nature; a wholeness; an understanding of the interconnectedness of all things. We had become blind to it. Capitalism made us lose sight of this fundamental reality, and the colonialists had been thorough, here, pushing capitalism's cold tentacles into every village and valley, turning people into labour, Eden into resources to be extracted.

'You can see something all around you and still not think it's right,' she says. 'We are not robots. We can think for ourselves.'

'But how could you prove it?'

She gives me a warm, wide smile. She's missing a few teeth.

'They could see how I lived. Subsistence farming, growing what I needed in the little yard in front. But there were testimonies too – from my children and grandchildren. They found it funny how I never lusted after the things that advertisers wanted me to lust after. Or what was that other kind of advertising? The people who were advertisers?'

'Influencers?'

'That's the one. My son would say things to me like "Don't you think that car's beautiful?" or "Don't you want to take a flight somewhere before you die?" and I would always reply, "Happiness comes from within, my boy."'

I finish my glass of water. 'Useful to have kids for those kinds of testimonies,' I say, 'so long as you don't have more than two!'

She laughs. 'I was lucky like that. I didn't plan it. I was too busy to have more children. That reminds me – you came about the orphanage.'

I shift in my seat. I pour myself another glass of water from the jug on the table. It's warm on my tongue. It will not quench my thirst. Hot air on my skin. 'Not really,' I say. 'Well, yes, that's why I'm going into the city, but I just came to ask if you would like to join the trip. If you have any business in town, or people you'd like to visit. You know, so the emissions are divided by a greater number of people.'

'But you work at the orphanage. That's why you're going?'

'Yes.'

'Those poor children.'

Her expression is impossible to read. Pity, of course, and sadness, but this could be a trap. She could be setting me up to test my loyalties. You hear stories about these informants all the time. The kind of people you'd least expect to be informants. Old women, for example, working as fronts for the young.

'We take good care of them,' I say.

'But don't you think the whole thing's barbaric?'

I look out of the window at the burnt, barren mountains. How wonderful it would feel to agree with her. A relief, to acknowledge the madness around us, to stop the madness getting in. Perhaps it's too late. I can't tell what's right or wrong any more. It *is* barbaric to kill people for having more than two children, for sure, but the planet can't sustain so many people and they should have known better. Is this the only path left? I know what the young people would say: there were other paths available to us. There were many other paths we could have taken. We chose not to take them, so this is all that's left.

'Ours is not to question the young,' I say.

The old woman clicks her tongue in irritation and leans back in her armchair. 'There are no young people here. You can see that.' But I can't see if there's anyone hiding behind the couch. I have no way of knowing if someone's waiting in the next room or listening in on this conversation from a control room somewhere. The young have eyes and ears everywhere.

'We are all Children of Gaia,' I say, and she sighs and rolls her eyes at me.

'We are all Children of Gaia,' she repeats.

She escorts me to her front door. 'Be kind to those orphans,' she says to me. 'There doesn't seem to be much space left for kindness any more.' She hands me my parasol. 'I won't be joining your little trip into town,' she says, 'but good luck.'

We are set to leave for the city at sunset. I have filled the bus with villagers and other staffers from the orphanage. A motley crew, mostly my age or older. Tattered clothes. Dust-streaked faces. They line the rows behind me in silence and stare out of the windows at the long, face-brick dormitories of the orphanage, which are almost beautiful in the fading red light. We must wait for the enforcer to make his way through the bus and capture everyone's identity on his tablet, before we can go. The enforcer is short, very thin, sickly almost, but he is young enough to be leadership in our district and so his power is absolute.

He stops at a woman in the second row with a baby on her lap. 'You,' he says, and she looks down at his feet. 'Yes, sir,' she says. Her voice is very small. The baby starts to niggle. She bounces her knee up and down to soothe it. Distracted, frightened.

'Do you know what my tablet is telling me?' he says.

The woman starts to cry. The person sitting next to her takes her hand.

'Please, sir,' she says. 'Please. I think I have enough. If I miscalculated, it was a mistake. It was an honest mistake.'

The enforcer laughs. He pats her on her head. 'Yes yes,

shhh. You can go to the city. But if you do, you will reach your emissions cap with this trip. If you want to come back, you will need to wait until next year.'

The woman wipes her eyes. 'That's fine, sir. I'm not coming back.'

He shakes his head and laughs again. 'What have you been doing this year to reach your limit so soon? Do you think you are more important than the rest of us? Do you think you deserve more?'

'No, sir.'

The enforcer exits the bus and I start the ignition. A loathsome sound, that filthy engine. Burning, burning while everything around us burns. I pull out onto the main road. The wind has come up again. The bus rocks with each gust from the southeast. Sand and dirt and little bits of rubbish blow across the road in thick clouds that make it difficult to see. Plastic bottles, from the time of recklessness, and detritus from the shacks that line the road. Something large comes loose and smacks into an old woman, knocking her face-first into the gravel. She struggles to get up as the wind howls around her. There are young people nearby, but they pretend not to see her. I turn left onto the freeway and accelerate through the dust.

Most of my passengers will visit relatives in the city. A few have come along to try to find supplies that we can't get out here in the mountains. And I will fetch a child to bring into our care. A child whose parents were locked up and starved to death. They were starved to make a point, the young people tell us, a point that still needs to be made because there are people who haven't changed their ways even now.

Darkness gathers in the valleys around us. A mercy extended by the shadow of the Earth. Faces turn black, and then the mountains and then at last the sky, slowly, imperceptibly, and soon the temperature will drop as the scorching sun moves west, away from us, to pour its fire down on what's left of the Americas. The only headlights on this freeway come from my own vehicle. The only lights in the villages nearby, candles or dim solar-powered bulbs, impossible to see from any distance.

I think about the Day of Judgement, when the grid was taken down and this pre-industrial gloom returned. We could see the stars again, that first night. It was beautiful, before we knew what was happening. Young saboteurs in the power plants. A coordinated attack throughout the country, throughout the world. The President was murdered in his sleep that night – by his own children. The presidents of so many countries were killed. They were our custodians, the young people said, and they had been derelict in their duties. All the directors and executives of companies that had failed to become carbon neutral by the deadline were rounded up the next morning. Suffocated to death in rooms pumped full of carbon monoxide and dioxide. Economists were arrested too, those who still preached the gospel of economic growth, anyway, and they were given the chance to publicly recant their views or face the firing squad. Everything is a circle, they were made to say, a closed system. Endless growth is the ideology of a cancer cell.

I think about the warning that the Children of Gaia gave us all, five years before then. When they set the deadline in the video that went viral because most people thought it was a joke. I can still see their leader, Linnea, in my mind's eye, fifteen years old at the time, only two years younger than I was. She was pale and sombre. Her hair was dirty, stringy, mousy brown. Dark clothes. Her voice quivered as she spoke, shaking with nervousness and rage.

'You have exactly five years,' she said, 'because that's how long we all have. We didn't set this deadline. You did. With your empty words and your inaction. We did not bring about the collapse of our living systems. You did. It'll be our problem, you said. The young can inherit this mess, after we've scraped a little more profit from the destruction first. But this is not a mess. It is suicide, and we won't stand by and let it happen. You have five years to change. We will be watching. The Children of Gaia are everywhere. We are in every home, on every street. We are watching to see what you do.'

My mother showed me the video on her phone. She thought the faux-terrorist aesthetic was funny. Harsh lighting, bare walls, heavy shadows. She thought the way Linnea took herself so seriously was funny. 'Teenagers should be worried about boyfriends and bitchy classmates,' she said.

'Well no, Mom, I think this is actually pretty serious.'

'*You're* not a Child of Gaia, are you?' she said, eyes wide with mock panic. 'In my own home!'

We laughed, then, and she ordered us chicken salads to be delivered for lunch. They arrived in their standard plastic takeaway bowls and she winked at me to seal the joke and cement our camaraderie. Linnea had said we shouldn't eat meat. We shouldn't use plastic. Shouldn't fly or get food delivered or buy clothes before the ones we were wearing fell apart. We shouldn't do any of the things that seemed so normal to us then. I remember gazing at that chicken breast in its plastic bowl and thinking how unremarkable it looked. How utterly lacking in planet-destroying drama. This whole thing is overblown, I remember thinking. This can't possibly make a difference.

We pull up to the orphan transfer centre on the outskirts of the city. The building is in darkness. The whole city's in darkness. Fires are burning in some of the shacks nearby and their dull orange glow illuminates the sandstorm around us. Sparks shoot past the windscreen in the howling gale. I step out into the street and take care not to tread on any bodies. The person might not be dead. They could just be sleeping. It's best not to look too closely.

There are no young people to greet me at the gate. No leaders or enforcers to check my security clearance. The building seems to be abandoned. Shutters slam against the window frames, over and over, in the wind. Many of the windows are broken. There's a child sitting on the front steps, hugging her knees against her chest. The main door is locked and bolted behind her.

'Are you the newly orphaned?' I say.

She looks up at me and nods.

'May they rest in peace.'

I offer her my hand and she stares at it without moving. 'I'm here to take you away from the city,' I say. 'Away from the city' is what we are supposed to call it. Not re-education or cleansing, not brainwashing. I shake my head. I mustn't think like this. It was the age of recklessness that brainwashed us. It was modernity. 'You'll like it there,' I say. There may even be some truth in that. It's certainly better than *this*.

Her eyes are wide and frightened. She won't take my hand.

'I'm sorry they did that to your parents,' I say. I look over her shoulder into the dark windows behind her. There are no young people to hear me. 'The sentencing is too harsh. They didn't deserve to die like that.'

'I'm an only child,' she says after a pause. Her voice is soft. I can barely hear her over the wind. 'They weren't sentenced. It wasn't a sentence.'

She hugs her knees tighter into her chest. 'What do you mean?' I say.

'My parents followed the rules. Look at this place. No one needs to starve us on purpose. There's nothing for anyone to eat.'

I must have the wrong child. I look to see if there is an enforcer anywhere. I look back towards the bus. None of the passengers have moved. They watch me from the illuminated cabin. Shadows staring out into the darkness and dust.

'Are there crops where you live?' the child says.

I think about the barren trenches in the untainted old woman's front yard. I think about the sweet, crisp apple in the hand of the leader who turned me away.

'There are, if you follow the rules,' I say.

She doesn't bother to respond. She knows as well as I do: the rules came too late.

The Lucky Ones

The first thing Andile did when he discovered the grey pube was pour himself a whiskey. The second thing he did was call Litha.

'I have a grey pube,' he said when Litha picked up.

'What time is it?'

'How can I have a grey pube when I'm not even thirty?'

Litha cleared his throat. His mattress creaked over the phone and a pillow thumped against the floor. Litha was sitting up in bed now, trying to think of something wise and comforting to say. Andile could wait. It's no big deal, Litha would say. It happens to everyone and no one speaks about it. It's just . . .

'Shit, friend,' Litha said, devastated.

. . . the beginning of the end.

'We're going out tonight,' Andile said. He hung up the phone.

On closer inspection it wasn't even grey. Grey sounded muted and respectful. It was white. Sun-bleached carcass-bone white. Dry driftwood white. The jeering, malicious white of pre-democratic presidents, insecure bosses, the drunk guys at rugby games who shout about racial quotas. The kind that belonged in the rubbish bin of history.

He seized the hair between his fingernails. Precision. A quick jerk of the hand. A tiny explosion of pain and the traitorous curl was out. It stuck to his finger, refused to go gently into that good toilet bowl, but he shook his hand and flicked his fingers wildly until it detached and drifted down into the water. Water restrictions be damned, he flushed it out of his life forever. He was a young man again. Dark and luxuriant.

A ping from his phone. *It's stress*, said the message from Litha. *Your spinster crotch has gone grey because you never let any boys near it.*

What did Litha know about that? He was never single. Always some young, adoring twink following him around. Andile tried not to think about the night he and Litha hooked up, years ago now but so often on his mind. Black-lit cubicle, glowing eyes and teeth, hope and excitement in Litha's face, like he couldn't believe how lucky he was to kiss Andile.

Andile downed his whiskey, found his car keys.

All of me went grey waiting for that joke, babe, he texted back.

At Zara in the Waterfront, Andile watched the sales assistant break away from the perimeter. She moved in for the kill, approaching with wide, smoky eyes and vacant helpfulness. He felt feral, malevolent, cornered. He knew what she was going to say. He recognised the movements: the troubled head-tilt, the uncertain kneading of hands.

'Sir?' she said, and he tried not to flinch. 'The men's department is through there.'

Andile dragged his cheeks into an exaggerated dead-eyed smile. Lowered eyebrows. Compressed forehead. It was his most withering expression. Meant to convey superiority, disdain, the end of his patience. 'Babes,' he said, 'I'm not looking for any men *right now*.'

The assistant retreated. Turned her charms to a friendlier set of customers, a mother-daughter combination with eyes on the florals.

Andile's eyes were on the jet black blouse with plunging neckline. He lifted it in both hands to catch the light. Fine gold crosses were sewn into the fabric with a single thread and all of it, even the blackness between the crosses, shimmered.

'I want to try this on,' he said to the woman guarding the changing rooms.

'The men's changing rooms are on the other side,' she said, her eyes bored and unfocused, eyelids heavy.

'What difference does it make? There's no one else here and—'

She lifted her arm as if it weighed a hundred kilos and pointed across the shop. Any other day Andile would have shouted at her, demanded to speak to the manager, given both of them a scathing, eloquent lecture on their complicity in toxic masculinity, their blinkers, the prison of gender performance, the first law of customer service which is that *the customer is always right*. But today was not that day. His white hair had spoken: he was elderly. His fight had fizzled out. He stormed across the shop, past the mother and daughter who pretended not to see him, under the big, silver back-lit sign that said MEN, past beige chinos and checked shirts, men buying things only for comfort or letting their wives decide what they should wear. A world of horror on that side of the barrier.

'He-hey, that's a woman's shirt,' laughed the men's changing room assistant.

Andile summoned his withering look, but his eyes were beginning to prickle. 'Do you not want my money?' he asked.

She shrugged and handed him a plastic number tag. 1. One times laughable item of clothing for the wrong sex.

'I'll let you know if I need a different size,' he said, using the last of his pride. He closed the door before she could tell him no and locked it behind him. He looked very small in the harsh neon strip-lighting, hunched in every one of the thousands of versions of himself repeating deep into the eternity of the mirror. He shook himself, stood up straight, lifted his chin. He pulled his T-shirt over his head and slipped into the blouse. He looked fucking fabulous in it.

'Yaaaaas kween!' said the white gay man waiting in line for the changing rooms when Andile came out to catwalk in front of the larger mirror. The man clicked his fingers and dipped, but Andile was in no mood for his solidarity.

Outside, in the sun, a marimba band was playing at the amphitheatre. There were traditional drummers just beyond the food court. In colourful dashikis and jaunty hats a brass band performed famous jazz numbers. All for the tourists, Andile knew, to make the atmosphere festive and loud, to match the Africa they expected: carefree and happy, a land of grinning musicians and sunshine and a wholesome, hearty attitude that triumphs over all adversity. There were tourists everywhere. Pink skin, blonde hair in dirty scrunchies. Floor-length black burqas. Dark-skinned West Africans with elaborate head wraps. Unknown languages skipped past Andile's ears. And the swallows: the Europeans who follow summer, half their lives in Germany or England and half their lives here, when the north is dark. They have a particular glow, the swallows. Deep tan and endless money. The glow of having escaped any kind of context.

Andile sat down on one of the concrete benches in the amphitheatre and placed his shopping bags beside him. He watched the tawdry marimba players. Lighting a cigarette, he contemplated inviting Litha to join him for lunch but Litha was probably busy. He watched a few stories on Instagram and, sure enough, there was Litha in the winelands with Andrew, the beautiful but boring guy he had been seeing for the last few weeks. Boomerangs of their chenin blanc, slender glasses clinking and retreating, clinking and retreating.

'I love your nails,' said a woman's voice next to Andile. She was young. Natural hair cut very short and barely combed out. Shapeless oversized t-shirt. Not the kind of person Andile expected to like his painted nails, but why was he making assumptions? He didn't know her inner life. Those judgemental shop assistants had got to him. Here he was imputing all kinds of Andrea from *The Devil Wears Prada* to this shabby young woman, as if she were trying to distance herself from the fashion industry and its whims and its gays, looking down on aesthetics and the shallow pleasures of self-expression. But she didn't dress that way because she was contemptuous of style. She was just poor.

'It's called "My Private Jet",' he said, spreading his fingers out so the black, glittery nail varnish could catch the sunlight.

'That's hilarious,' she said.

'Babes, closest I'll ever come to one.'

She smiled at him and turned back to the marimba band. 'Don't you love it here?' she said.

Andile exhaled a few lazy smoke rings. He liked her. He didn't want to seem a snob. 'It's okay,' he said.

She half-laughed, half-clicked her tongue at him. 'You're very lucky,' she said. 'I save up to come here. There's nothing where I live.'

He didn't need to ask where she lived. It was all over her, the sprawling, sandy wasteland on the outskirts of the city. Apartheid's hell-scar.

'Andile,' he said, and she took his hand.

'Nompilo.'

He offered her a cigarette.

'No, thanks,' she said, 'I want to keep my lungs.' But she didn't say it with malice. She was teasing him, giving him the side-eye.

'Which band is your favourite?' he asked, pointing his eyes towards the musicians. He meant the question as an apology for his bougie ingratitude, an encouragement for her to talk about what she loved, but it came out sounding patronising: look at your little musicians. She closed up. Smiled at him again but left. She walked down to the front of the amphitheatre, small and shy, but then began to dance. She closed her eyes, stretched out her arms and swooped them around her in figures of eight. Andile's mouth was sour. He finished his cigarette. Nompilo was hunched over now with balled up fists, bicycling her arms to the rhythm of the marimbas. The band cheered and broke into a call and response, their movements growing more boisterous, lifting their mallets high above their heads and thumping them down harder and faster, louder, quicker, building to a dramatic crescendo of sweat and smiles and chanting and cheering and thundering drumbeats. Nompilo exploded into the shape of a star, arms and legs outstretched, fingers shaking.

She was a bit odd, this woman, but she sure knew how to squeeze some joy from the moment. A few muted claps from the tourists. Most of them looked bored, even if this spontaneous dancer was exactly the kind of Africa they got on a plane for.

Andile thought of Nompilo that night in the club. He wore his obsidian black blouse and his gold earrings and gold eyeshadow and a purse and they were the same, the two of them. She wasn't intimidated by a world designed to keep her out. Expensive shops. Privatised public space. Right of Admission Reserved. She took her shoddy clothes and her poverty and she danced it all freely in front of the people who like to pretend she doesn't exist. He was doing the same, or trying to at least. Existing without apology. Refusing to believe he doesn't belong. The masc-for-masc, bearded, muscled gays looked him up and down like he was a circus act, desperate to prove to themselves and each other that they were no different from the straight men who hated them, no weaker. They devoured Andile with their cold eyes of judgement. He lifted his chin to meet their gaze.

'I hear you've got a grey pube!' someone bellowed in his ear. Andrew, red-cheeked and sweaty. Litha stood behind him in the flashing lights and hip hop, eyes wide with amusement.

'I hear you've finally started getting some pubes of your own!' Andile replied. An easy joke to make. Andrew was . . . what? Twenty-two at the most. Andile mocked Litha about it relentlessly. Is he old enough to go out with us? When is his curfew? Does his mom know he's fraternising with homosexuals?

But Andile didn't feel like making jokes tonight. Didn't feel like talking at all. He wished Andrew wasn't there. Wished he could get a moment alone with Litha, deep in the club where it was too dark to see his friend's eyes, to think about whether he could live up to the expectation. Would he kiss him? Probably not, even this time around, even after all these years.

Andile left them at the bar. On the dance floor, where the music was too loud for conversation, he waved to other friends. Blew kisses, took some videos for Insta. In seconds, the comments came in:

You're so fierce.

Flames!

Slay!

You give me life!

Andile shimmied his shoulders and pouted his lips. He wanted to connect with the joy he'd seen on Nompilo's face when she danced. He kept dancing long after everyone he knew had left, friends pairing up or going home in threes. He winked at Litha and Andrew when they squeezed past him on their way out. 'I'll be fine here, babes, they're playing my song!' He didn't need sex to feel free.

You get home okay, love?

Litha's message woke Andile up. Heavy headed, he dragged himself to the bathroom. Makeup off. Into the shower. No new nasty surprises this time. No harbingers of age and decline. He got dressed quickly. Plain white collared shirt. Jeans. Tight but not too tight. Birthday card, nicely wrapped book, bottle of MCC from the fridge. He was late for lunch at his parents' house. His dad's fifty-eighth birthday. He lost another ten minutes removing "My Private Jet".

Cars ramped up on the pavements on both sides of the Plumstead street, under the plane trees, in the drive. The house would be full: cousins, aunts, uncles, his father's old friends from work and church. Andile turned on the charm, greeted everyone with a smile and a joke. He went through to the kitchen to put the bubbles in the fridge. His headache was mounting a ruthless attack.

'You look terrible, Andile,' Zanele said.

'It's good to see you too, Little Sis.'

Zanele laughed and gave him a hug. She smelt of shea butter and ylang-ylang, wholesome and clean. It made him feel vile and contaminated, as if the club was still all over his skin.

'He's just hungover,' said Akhona, their elder sister. She stopped slicing cucumber. 'He's always hungover,' she added with theatrical disapproval.

'I am not hungover. How *very* dare you.'

'Can I pour you a drink, then?' she said.

'I'm never drinking again.'

Zanele rolled her eyes. Akhona went back to making her salad. She had loved going out with Andile when they were younger. Loved having a cool, gay brother to take her to places she had never heard of, places where the men left her alone, or partied with her and made her laugh and expected nothing in return. 'I miss my single life,' she'd told him only a few weeks ago, her voice a little sadder than she intended. 'Is that a terrible thing to say?' She loved her husband and Xolani, her son, but he'd brought a deadening monotony with him. 'Boiling vegetables. Stacking blocks. Cutting toast into little squares,' she'd recited off her fingers. She never had time to talk to her husband, or anyone else for that matter, about adult, non-motherly things. Would she never get to enjoy the surprising delight of a stranger's company again? Where were the opportunities for unexpected connection?

'You do look odd, though,' Akhona said. 'Is this your middle-management-on-the-weekend look? You didn't have to disguise yourself for Dad.'

Andile sat on the counter between them. He inserted a cherry tomato into his mouth. 'I'm just trying to ease him into *how* gay I am.'

Xolani came running into the kitchen. He hugged Akhona's legs and gave Andile a shy wave. 'Hello, Uncle.'

'How's my favourite?' Andile said. 'Does your mom know I'm stealing you?' He grabbed Xolani and pulled him up onto his lap.

'You can't steal me!' Xolani giggled. Buried his face in Andile's shoulder.

'I promise I'll still come visit you guys,' Akhona said, trying to keep a serious face.

'Just remember to pack all your toys because I'm never giving you back,' said Andile.

'Nooooo!' Xolani whined.

'We're joking, my darling,' Akhona said, stroking his chin. Xolani wrapped his arms around Andile's neck and kissed him on the cheek. It was then, looking over Xolani's head, that Andile saw Neo standing in the doorway. How long had he been there? Why wasn't he moving?

'Hello, Tata,' Andile said. 'It's nice to see you again.'

Neo stepped into the room. He had become, in the years since Andile had seen him, an old man. His eyes were hooded. The hair at his temples was grey. He walked across the kitchen. Heavy, Big Man walk. Unflattering beige golf shirt. Stomach out, shoulders back. He opened the fridge and, while staring into it, facing away from them all he said, 'It's good to see you too, Andile.'

His voice had that high-pitched, raspy quality that some elderly men get. Andile had thought Neo and Dad were the same age, best friends. But it was obvious now that Neo was at least ten years his father's senior.

Neo turned around with his beer and stood silent for a while, watching them. Then he said, 'So it's true, you are one of those who likes men.'

Akhona stopped chopping. Andile could hear his own breathing.

Eventually, he replied, 'Only the nice ones, Tata.'

'And the nice ones are hard to find,' Zanele said. She clapped her hands and shrugged, opening her palms to reveal emptiness. Andile could have kissed her. Akhona laughed, resumed chopping. Andile smiled at the old man. Conversation over.

But not for Neo. 'You know,' he said, 'there was no one like that when I was your age.'

Akhona put down her knife. 'Tata,' she said, 'there were. You just didn't know them.'

Neo took a sip of his beer. 'What I'm saying is – it was not allowed.'

Andile could hear those now-famous words in his uncle's remark, the threats of an old president: when I was growing up, a gay man would not have stood in front of me. I would have knocked him out. Andile would not allow himself to feel afraid. He could handle himself in an argument. He knew to expect hatred like this from old people. He could stand his ground. He did it with shop assistants and telemarketers, with hecklers in the street and church ministers and the casually racist, thoughtlessly homophobic people he worked with. He did it in online neighbourhood-watch groups, on Twitter, with friends of friends at picnics in Kirstenbosch. Why was he so nervous now?

He passed Xolani to Akhona and got down off the counter. Standing between his sisters, working hard to keep his voice steady, he said: 'We can be as gay as we like now, Tata. We can kiss and marry and sprinkle rainbows all over town. I'm sure it's very hard for you.'

The deep chuckle that came from Neo's throat made Andile's blood run cold.

'You're very lucky,' his uncle said.

'Let's go find Gogo,' Andile said, taking Xolani in his arms again and carrying him outside to where his mother and his aunts were lounging by the pool.

The party was still in full swing when Andile excused himself. His hangover had not subsided, not even after a Stoney and a huge helping of oxtail. Flies were swooping lazily through the sweltering afternoon. His young cousins were splashing in the pool. Gleeful screams as their uncles and fathers threw them into the air then decided, without warning, that it was enough and returned to their beers. If the family is big enough, the continuity is never broken. This was just like his own childhood: the Sundays in summer, the oxtail, the pool, the grumpy older men. Except now he was the uncle. And pain throbbed at his temples, adult and self-inflicted. It flared every time he moved his eyes too quickly.

He closed the door of his parents' bedroom and sprawled on their soft white bed. Laughter, the dull bass of music coming from the living room down the passage. He was happy as he set the alarm on his phone for twenty minutes and closed his eyes.

The door clicked shut. Locked. 'Ma?' said Andile, sitting up. It was Neo.

'I wanted to see you,' the old man said.

Could he hit Neo with the lamp, maybe? Was there a knife in his mother's bedside drawer? Andile scanned the room for anything he could use to defend himself. He was too thin, too effeminate. Neo could overpower him easily, even at his age. But surely he wouldn't attack his best friend's son in his own home?

Neo was approaching. Andile folded his arms around his knees. He could run now. Duck around the old man, flee to safety. But Neo's movements were halting, almost nervous. He sat down slowly at the foot of the bed. 'I want to tell you something,' he said.

'Okay.'

'I think it's good you're so open with your family.'

'Okay.'

'They love you, in spite of everything.'

Andile pressed his thumbs into his eye sockets to relieve the last of the headache. They didn't love him in spite of anything. They just loved him. His thumbs came away with the faintest dusting of gold eye shadow on their prints. A deep, throaty chortle in the living room. Andile's mom. Her scandalised, conspiratorial laugh. Someone had told an inappropriate joke.

'You're very lucky.'

Again with the luck. He'd said it in the kitchen. Nompilo said it at the Waterfront. Akhona said it to him all the time.

'You what-whats have rights now.'

Was it lucky not to be persecuted? Or was it just the basic fucking minimum requirement of what it meant to be a human being? Straight people didn't go around feeling grateful all the time for not being attacked in the street. And he wasn't lucky. He still felt unsafe, often. He still felt lonely almost all of the time. And ashamed. Part of him was always ashamed. Gay rights haven't fixed everything, Andile wanted to shout, but what would this old man understand about that?

'Yes,' was all he said.

'I have not been so lucky,' said Neo. He looked up and held Andile's gaze until Andile understood. The room suddenly lost its anchoring, swerved and dipped like a boat out at sea. His father's oldest friend, the uncle at all of their family events, the no-nonsense maths teacher and argumentative soccer coach. The guy who wore beige golf shirts, for Christ's sake. And Andile had never suspected.

'Your father can never know.'

'I'm sure he'd be okay with it,' Andile said, holding the mattress as the room stabilised. He was back on dry land. 'He was fine with me. He tries to understand.'

'I have been lying to him all our lives.'

Had he lied? There had never been a wife, never even a girlfriend as far as Andile knew. There were other clues too: Neo's obvious discomfort when people asked him when he was planning to get married, when they included him in their discussions about beauties on TV. His tendency to get maudlin at big family celebrations. He'd wept like Akhona was his own daughter when she graduated from university.

'You had to, Tata. Everything was different then.'

Neo said nothing. Suddenly Andile's neck felt hot. He did not want this weight on his soul. This old man's suffocating secret. A life of secrecy and shame, darkness and half-truths and diversions. The only scraps of affection he got were from nephews, cats, friends, and even the friends could never know him, not really. They had families of their own, people more important, more genuinely loved. How could anyone bear this? Andile closed his eyes. Don't make me carry it.

'I've only been with prostitutes,' Neo went on, relentless. 'People I knew would never turn up when—'

'Why are you telling me this?' Andile said, surprised at the hostility in his own voice. He was sorry he asked. He didn't want to hear the answer which was, so obviously, just so that Neo could finally tell *someone*.

'Because . . . ' said Neo. 'I don't know. I think, because you are so beautiful.'

Andile cleared his throat. He didn't follow the logic. 'Thank you,' he said at last.

Neo lunged towards him. Big Man heaviness on Andile's chest. Dry, cracked lips. Coarse stubble. The beige shirt smelt faintly sour, of damp laundry not properly dried. Neo's breath was sweet and stale, a mix of beer and oxtail. Strong hands tightened their grip on Andile's neck. 'It's fine,' Neo mumbled into Andile's mouth, 'relax.' Andile shoved hard against Neo.

'Fuck!'

'I'm sorry.' Neo couldn't look at him.

Andile's muscles were tight, tingling. He pushed up off the bed and paced the room. He wanted to punch a hole in the wall, like they did in the movies. Scream at this miserable old man.

'I'm sorry,' Neo said again. His cheeks were wet and he would not look up from his hands in his lap. 'I'm so sorry.'

Andile watched Neo's powerful chest heave in ragged, jerky breaths. He looked at the hair at the man's temples. Thousands of short, tightly curled strands. White as an epiphany. He stopped pacing. Leaning towards the old man, he took his face in his hands and kissed him. A long, soft, passionate kiss.

'I'm not doing that again,' he said when they pulled apart. His hands were wet from Neo's tears. 'But if you like, Tata, we can go for lunch sometime. Or coffee. We can talk. I'm here.'

A knock on the bedroom door. 'Come on, you two,' said Andile's mother. 'We're about to cut the cake. Your dad's going to need some help blowing out the candles.'

Andile watched the little flames go out, two or three at a time, his father's puffed cheeks and watering eyes behind them. A little O formed between his lips. Fifty-eight years was a lot of history to extinguish. His father smiled at Andile. A wide, happy, unselfconscious smile. He loved being surrounded by his family, his wife and three children, his friends and sisters and cousins. It was a life he was proud of. In the suburbs too. Unimaginable when he was young. Unimaginable, such a simple thing as this.

Andile pinched a few of the smoking wicks, got up to pour himself a glass of MCC. No one else wanted any, not even his sisters, not Neo, brooding and quiet in the rust-coloured armchair. Not the birthday boy, who had switched from beer to rooibos because he thought it went better with cake.

Andile squeezed in between Zanele and Akhona on the couch. 'I'm glad you escaped the kitchen,' Akhona whispered. 'I had no idea Neo was such a bigot.'

Andile let the chocolate sweetness of the birthday cake sit for a moment on his tongue.

'He's not so bad,' he said. 'He just doesn't know how to talk about it.'

He messaged Litha during a break in the conversation.

We're going for a drink tonight, he said.

And then, because he was feeling lucky, a minute later he added: *Just the two of us, please. I've got something I want to tell you.*

The King of the Jungle

Laughter wakes Nombulelo from dreamless black sleep. Little girls, somewhere outside the shack. She looks into the darkness. She tries to return to sleep. She can't sleep, but she's too tired to get up. She's always tired. Ma'Khumalo says old people don't need much sleep, but what does she know? Ma'Khumalo has boundless energy. Singing at church never wears her down. Township gossip at tea afterwards doesn't make her ache. Her unwavering faith energises her. The two of them are not old in the same way.

Nombulelo heaves the blankets off her chest and sits up. The cold air feels wet on her skin. It loosens the phlegm in her lungs. She coughs. Her ribs hurt. Girls laugh outside, again, as they make their way to school. Footsteps crunch along the path. The empty sounds of the living.

She strikes a match and light flickers up from the lamp, dirty and orange. Darkness eases into solid, ordinary things: a white mini fridge with a portable electric hotplate on top; an old desk with peeling wood-effect linoleum. At the foot of her bed a lumpy, olive green couch and beside it, on the floor, a plastic washbasin and Thembi's crate filled with dolls, crayons and the grubby soft tiger toy she loved so much.

There's mieliepap in the pot which Nombulelo heats, along with a cup of sweet, milky tea to help with the headache. The radio is playing one of her favourite hymns. A month ago the words would have made her angry but now she's too tired to feel anything. She ignores the words, hums along to the melody. It still soars, still has a little magic in it, almost lets her believe we're all part of something greater.

A voice outside the door. 'Morning, Mama. Is there anything I can get for you in town?'

It is her neighbour, Eunice.

Nombulelo clicks her tongue in irritation. She needs kerosene and a tin of apricot jam, but in her wallet she finds nothing but a crumpled photo of Thembi on her last birthday. Smiling over a piece of rainbow cake. A smear of icing on her cheek. 'I'm fine,' she shouts back. 'Go. You'll miss your train.'

She sits on the couch and begins massaging her swollen ankles. Her hand bumps against an unseen bottle of brandy on the floor. It teeters then falls, the clanging glass announcing to all who care to listen that Nombulelo is a shameful person. Pathetic and weak. She grabs hold of the neck. Did Eunice hear it? If she heard it she'll tell Ma'Khumalo. Ma'Khumalo will come by again. Press her lips together in that sour, sanctimonious way of hers, and tell her to have faith. The Lord is watching over her. Nombulelo wraps the bottle in a plastic bag and hides it under the couch. Drinking is for gangsters and tsotsis with no morals, for those who abandon their families and waste all their money on themselves. She does not drink. She is not a drinker.

*

Gary can't sleep. He rolls away from Mike so the light from his cellphone doesn't wake him, and he checks Twitter again. #MandelaDay is trending already. Is that a good thing? People are interested, at least. Gary and his team will be 'part of the conversation' this year, just as he promised his boss. Today's a small thing, barely a drop in the marketing budget, but Gary had argued hard for it. It's a good thing to do, he'd said, but now his idealism feels heavy. Every other bright-eyed millennial brand manager in the country is doing the same thing, trying to splice philanthropy together with brand building. How will his team's good deeds be any different from the rest?

He slips out of bed and makes his way to the kitchen. It's about emotional engagement, he reminds himself as he puts on the kettle, not exposure. Their customers will love that they're giving back. Even if they don't tell their friends about it, even if it doesn't go viral, those who see his school makeover project will become more loyal to the brand. He stares at the sea for a while. It's the same dark grey as the granite countertops, as the sky. The kettle flicks off, losing its blue glow as the water comes to rest. He's overthinking the whole thing.

Gary takes his coffee to the living room and fires up his laptop. Bronwyn and Chantelle have sent him photos of themselves loading paints and rollers and T-shirts into Bron's car last night. In one, they're standing on either side of the open boot with manic grins and raised thumbs. It's a great pic. Gary shares it from all of the brand's social media accounts and uploads it to the campaign page he set up for today.

Mike stumbles in, wiping sleep from his eyes. 'Thank God it stopped raining, hey? Would have made your kumbaya, save-the-world-one-school-at-a-time day a mess.'

Gary looks to the heavens. 'Didn't you have a meeting to get to?'

Mike grins and kisses him on the forehead. He's infuriatingly pleased with himself. 'I'm playing, baby. You're a legend for making this happen. Can I make you some eggs?'

*

There isn't much jam left in the tin, so Nombulelo spreads it thin. She has enough bread for five sandwiches. She packs them into a plastic supermarket packet and heads for the taxi rank. She can't face the walk to school today.

Everyone with a job is standing in line in the early-morning fog. It's the busiest time of day, draining the township into the city. This was Nombulelo's life every day until a few months ago when the family she cleaned for moved to Australia. They said they'd find her another job, but her age must have counted against her. No one wanted a cleaner who took all morning just to vacuum the house.

A young man shifts to make room for Nombulelo in a taxi and she thanks him, but the music in his headphones is so loud he doesn't hear her. Beside him, a woman sits with a small girl on her lap, hiding and revealing herself from behind her hands to squeals of delight. Nombulelo fixes her eyes on the road ahead. When the driver's music comes on it's a relief. It rattles the windows and shakes her chest. No small talk, no giggles from the child, no thoughts.

'Thirteen, Gogo,' shouts the collector over the din.

'I'm only going down the road.'

'Fine. Give me five.'

She takes out her wallet and remembers, before she opens it, that there is nothing inside. She holds the wallet in her lap and pretends to count out change as warmth spreads from her neck into her cheeks. The other passengers pass their fare forward. The conductor makes change and passes it back. Perhaps she will be overlooked.

'It's five rand, Gogo,' he says again. He is wearing sunglasses even though the sun is lost behind cloud.

'Can I give you a sandwich?' she says at last.

The driver pulls onto the side of the road and stops. 'Get out,' he says. She is barely out of the taxi before the other passengers start gossiping. The young man takes his headphones off and shouts something at her, but she is not going to listen. She does not need to hear his abuse. Doesn't he have anything better to do? Why does everyone always have an opinion on how she must live her life? Go back to church. Talk to people. Try to move on. What do any of them know? Ma'Khumalo was the worst of them. 'Don't spend all your money on city doctors,' she said when Thembi first got sick, 'they do the same thing as the nurses at the clinic.' As if the nurses at the clinic hadn't given Thembi aspirin tablets and sent her home. Aspirin tablets!

The man with the headphones catches up to her and grabs her shoulder. She tries to focus on his face, the words leaving his mouth. He tells her he's paid her fare. Then he gives her a twenty rand note. She takes it before she realises what's happening, and then tries to give it back. He refuses. 'God bless you,' she says, an old impulse. He smiles at her with surprising warmth as they get back into the taxi. 'We have to make our own blessings, Gogo.'

The taxi sets off again. Nombulelo stares out of the window at the shacks and washing lines flying by, the rows of concrete outhouses and skinny dogs and puddles of sewerage and rain. Nothing ever changes. Even the people look the same as when Nombulelo moved to the city. Hopeless and broken. But they aren't the same people. They are young and unemployed and the people Nombulelo first saw on these streets must have grown old by now. They're sitting on their beds at home, perhaps. Or they're in the ground.

She gets out at the school, a small compound of single-storey buildings the colour of a rotten tooth. There are boys kicking a soccer ball around in the yard of one of the new housing projects beside the freeway. She had promised Thembi they would live in one of these developments one day, with running water and brick walls, like white people. 'We'll be kings!' Thembi had said, thrusting her tiger plushie into the air. 'You can be the main king, granny, but I also get to be one.'

Nombulelo tries to hand out her sandwiches at the school gates. No one will take them.

'We have lunch today, Gogo,' says one of the girls.

'They brought us food,' says another, gesturing to the group of people unpacking paints in the quad.

A third girl takes out some change and offers it to Nombulelo and Nombulelo realises, with a sick feeling in her stomach, that the girl is Ma'Khumalo's granddaughter, following instructions.

'I don't want your money,' she snaps. Then she tries to smile. She will not get angry. Not today. They are painting the giant tiger on the wall for Thembi. The tiger she loved so much. A small piece of her will live on.

'Are you okay, Gogo?' the girl says. Nombulelo puts a hand on her shoulder and waits for the dizziness to pass. It's punishment for last night, she knows, but she can't afford to be dizzy today. She excuses herself and makes her way to the bathrooms in Block C. She closes the cubicle door and takes out a small bottle from her skirt. The first sip singes her tongue, her throat, her stomach. The second sip is gentler. She sits for a moment on the closed toilet seat and breathes.

The third sip is warm and forgiving. It soothes the tremors in her hands. A benediction for her tired heart.

*

Gary turns down the volume in his car – it's his *Songs To Sing In The Shower* playlist and it's perfect for getting him in the right mood for today, but the offramp is coming up and he's been blasting it far too loud. He switches into the slow lane. So good to see another new housing project go up. This one has three-storey units, angular lines and earthy tones of orange and brown – a distinctly African aesthetic, the kind he is always telling Mike to design. Mike's architecture practice builds houses that look like they're from Scandinavian magazines – all planes of glass and textured wood. What relevance does that have? Gary checks the sign but he can't find the architect credit.

He reads *This City Works For You*, then has to take the turn. He exits the freeway. Makes sure his doors are locked.

At the school, Bronwyn and Chantelle are distributing T-shirts – green and white to match the brand colours. Gary snaps a few pics of the kids pulling them on, then wanders around the school taking photos of all the grotty buildings. The walls are cracked and peeling and filthy. These will make great before-and-after pics for the campaign page.

'We'd like to give a warm welcome to our sponsors and thank them from the bottom of our hearts,' the headmaster says when Gary gets back to the quad. 'We know there are many communities in need and we appreciate that you chose to work with us.' The learners cheer and clap and Gary gets a great shot of some of the younger ones raising their hands in the air like they're at church and the spirit has taken them.

When Gary first called the headmaster about his Mandela Day plan he said he also wanted to do something playful for the younger kids. They agreed all the buildings would be green and white to keep Gary's boss happy, to keep the brand front and centre, but the nursery school block would get a mural. They decided on a jungle scene and as Gary approaches the block now, he sees the outline has already been sketched onto the wall. It looks fantastic. Huge ferns and banana trees, big cats, a giraffe. It's childlike but not ugly. Authentic but with good composition.

He sets up his laptop in one of the classrooms. The kids outside start singing a Beyoncé song and he hears Chantelle and Brad and Siya join in. He closes his eyes and tries to take in the moment, to be truly present for this. No fussing over social media analytics and the perfect copy for the campaign. No worrying about what everyone is saying on Twitter. He listens to the singing. This is what makes it all worth doing.

When he goes outside again an old woman is painting with the kids. She's not wearing their branded T-shirt and she looks like she might be homeless.

'Her granddaughter died,' says the headmaster, reading

his eyes. 'The child was in the nursery school, so we thought it would be nice to include her. I'll ask her to leave.'

'Don't do that,' Gary says. She should be part of it. It's a nice gesture. A little weird but that's the cultural chasm he's working to bridge. Life in the townships is messy and he can learn to embrace the mess.

'Smile!' he says, and snaps a few action shots.

'Excuse me,' he says to the old woman, 'can you smile, please?'

She does not smile. When she looks at him it's as if he's been punched in the chest, as if she loathes everything about him. He goes for a walk to resuscitate his excitement. He videos some of the kids, applauds the completion of Block B. When he gets back to the nursery school the old woman is slopping orange paint all over the place.

'Everyone? Everyone! Stop for a second, please. Thanks. So our brand is about being the Africa experts and so we've gotta make sure the picture is of African animals. Okay? We're in Africa, guys. Let's celebrate it!' His voice lets him down. Makes him sound like every patronising old white guy he grew up hating. 'Lions, giraffes, rhinos all good,' he continues, trying to power through how uncomfortable he feels, 'but no tigers, okay?'

The old woman shouts something but the learners distract her. 'I'm so sorry, Gary,' the headmaster says, cringing and fussing in a way that Gary finds even more unnerving – the man is at least twenty years older than he is – 'I didn't think!

Of course, we all know the brand tagline. How about a lion? Shall we make it a lion?'

'Sounds good.'

The headmaster turns to the kids. 'Let's give this jungle a king!'

The painting resumes and the woman slops more orange paint against the wall. She sways from side to side. A learner near her tries to take her brush away but she won't let it go. She shoves him and gets paint all over his T-shirt. Gary takes out his phone to message Mike. What should he do? Why does there have to be a scene? Is it such a big deal to paint a fucking lion?

The headmaster whispers something in the old woman's ear and she screams 'No!' She starts to sing. It sounds like a hymn but she's forgotten the words. Just a mumble of swallowed sounds. She's clearly drunk. The headmaster reaches for her shoulder; she shakes him off, stumbles backwards and falls onto the ground, sending mini brandy bottles tumbling out of her skirt's pocket and knocking over a tin of paint, which spills over her legs and feet. He lifts her by the armpits and drags her to the gates. She fights and shouts and the children try not to watch.

Once locked out, the woman sings from the side of the road. Gary can't make sense of the slurred words but her voice is almost beautiful. It soars and retreats, masterful and impassioned and dignified, like it's forgotten to whom it belongs, like she is not this crumpled, broken thing.

'I hope this isn't what you remember from today,' the headmaster says, 'and you come back again in the future.' Gary smiles at him and tries to remember why he's here. The kids get a brighter, cleaner school. The marketing team gets to do something meaningful. He can recite the reasons to himself but he no longer feels them. Perhaps the problem is he isn't participating enough.

He picks up a paint brush and helps with the baobab tree. The lion starts to take shape beside him. The kids have finished its giant orange mane. They have covered its stripes with a thick coat of yellow. The drunk woman's distant singing gets softer. She breaks and resumes a few times, and then she stops. She rises to her feet, stiff and slow, and shuffles down the street, leaving a lopsided trail of orange paint in the dirt.

Gary checks the ground for the little bottles, but someone has tidied them away already. Those don't need to be in the pictures.

Boy Meets Boy

I

Carl and Jack meet in the hot tub of a sex club in a part of town that neither of them has been to before, all homelessness and stains on the walls. Carl is there because he followed his ex, Tom, in the hope of seducing him in a darkroom, using his post-breakup body to trick Tom into falling back in love with him. Jack is there because he's never had sex with a man and he doesn't want his first time to be with someone he loves. He wants it to be meaningless and perfunctory and to get it over with so that he can go into his first relationship with a level head – the head of someone who knows what to expect, who to trust and how to avoid infatuation.

Carl and Jack fall in love, but not right there in the swirling tank of chlorine and semen; later, once they've texted to meet up in clothes and had gin and tonics together and taken a weekend away up the coast where they discover that they both love Margaret Atwood. Contrary to his plan, Jack's first time ends up being with someone he loves. It hurts like hell and that corroborates a hunch he's had for a while about the connection between physical pain and intimacy. He begs Carl to treat him like the bullies at school treated him. Carl says he wants no part in that degradation. He thinks it's unlike the healthy relationships he has seen, but really it is just a different kind of degradation from the quiet, slow erosion of mutual respect that he knows from watching his own parents' marriage. Carl and Jack break up.

Carl marries Tom, the ex he was stalking the night he met Jack, though he never tells Tom the story of that night and how he was watching him from the shadows and masturbating in the tub.

II

Carl meets Tom many years before, in the once upon a time of university. Tom has only recently accepted that he likes boys and finds Carl's attention empowering. Carl is masculine and dark, with muscular forearms that trigger a strange combination of envy and lust. Tom feels sexy and virile and hopeful that there is a whole world beyond the camp, desexualised gay people he sees on TV. He enjoys having Carl around but there is a niggling doubt that presses down on his chest whenever Carl says things like 'we' or 'our plans this weekend' to their mutual friends. Love is supposed to be blind and Tom is not blinded. He can see Carl's faults as clearly as if they were his own, and while they don't all irritate him, he doesn't find them quirky and adorable either. Tom tells Carl he'd like to take things slow. Carl tells Tom he's happy with any arrangement so long as Tom stays in his life. This feels cloying and desperate and makes Tom lose all respect for Carl, but it also makes him hate himself a little when he ends the relationship. What kind of person is disgusted by love?

Carl refuses to answer any of Tom's calls but Tom sees him often at the gym. Carl is always at the gym, mouthing along to the Alanis Morissette lyrics streaming through his headphones while he sprints on the treadmill at 15 kmph. Carl sweats. Tom goes to yoga. Tom would like to better understand his own desires and motivations. He does not want to go through life hurting the people who love him. He begins meditating on Monday and Thursday nights at a studio downtown where Jack also meditates. Tom and Jack go to the same class on Thursdays, they sit quite close to one another and they smile whenever they catch each other's eye, but they never actually meet.

Tom decides he likes Aaron, the guy who leads the meditation class. Aaron has been to India and has practised meditation for many years. He is comfortable with his sexuality and makes Tom feel less frightened of himself when they talk. Aaron and Tom begin dating, which Tom is particularly proud of because Aaron is a little feminine and this means that Tom has made progress in combating his internalised homophobia. Their sex is disappointing but this is the price of a well-adjusted emotional life. Aaron seldom wants to have sex, and when he does he always wants to be fucked. At first this makes Tom feel powerful but then it makes him feel hollow and bored, trapped in a role that wasn't written for him. He realises he is not attracted to Aaron, though he likes him as a friend and hopes they can stay in touch. Aaron takes the break up well and, because he is such a spiritual and easy-going guy, agrees to be friends with Tom. Tom finds a new meditation group and goes for increasingly awkward platonic coffee dates with Aaron. He begins to understand that he has no interest in being friends with Aaron. If he is honest with himself, which he is trying to be these days, he sees Aaron only because he likes to think of himself as a good person, a nice person, but really he just lacks the courage to disappoint people.

Tom goes on to have four relationships in six months and begins to worry that he will never find someone who feels right. He starts going to sex clubs so that he can stop over-thinking it. He has wild sex with perfect strangers, both on the giving and the receiving end, and he feels high on adrenaline for a few weeks. He is alive. He is uninhibited. He contracts genital warts. Tom applies the cream and decides it was foolish to break up with Carl. Carl's body is much improved since they broke up, thanks to all that time at the gym, but his company still leaves Tom feeling quietly sad. Tom decides that this is the human condition. It's immature to fight it.

Carl and Tom marry on a cliff overlooking the ocean. Both of their mothers wear blue.

III

Jack, who doesn't have a mother (she died of a particularly virulent form of cancer that took four months to do its work), kills himself at twenty-eight. He swallows a drum of sleeping pills in gulps of five or six and turns up the Mozart on his phone so that his death can feel momentous. Blackness gathers slowly and then quite suddenly and in the split second before his consciousness cuts out, a clear hope forms. It's an immense hope, infinite almost, from millions of years of rising up in the final moments of every living thing. The hope that there is something out there, that the end isn't really the end. I will survive my death. There has been some point to my life. It's not just a succession of circumstances and the ability to perceive them. For the briefest moment this hope triumphs over the laws of physics and Jack's mother is there. There is light and warmth. She makes him the lamb stew he used to love and she understands why he couldn't tell her all the things that mattered most. She sees his shame and his self-hatred and his doubt, the tormentors at school and the late-night prayers to be straight and the sitting alone in his flat night after night after Carl broke up with him. She sees how afraid he was that she, too, couldn't love him if she knew who he really was, and this knowledge heals everything. She is no longer angry that he pushed her away. There is atonement in these final spasms of dying neurons. They almost embrace.

The boys who bullied Jack at school hear about his death in an alumni email that gets sent out once a quarter. By then the soft parts of Jack's face have partially dissolved, but the hard bones of his skull remain, and this happens out of sight, in the earth, like the foundations of a building. One of the bullies tells his wife, 'Huh, I went to school with that guy.' Another remembers teasing Jack and turns on the rugby to take his mind off it. Of course the bullying wasn't why Jack did it. It's been years since they were kids.

Carl hears about the suicide from a mutual friend. He wants to attend the funeral but feels too ashamed to do so. He tells Tom that an ex-boyfriend killed himself and Tom says he doesn't remember anyone called Jack. We didn't go out for long, Carl says, just a few months when you and I were broken up. Tom hugs Carl. Carl wants to say that he saw it coming, but when he opens his mouth to speak it feels disloyal, and it feels like a lie.

He says he is going to buy orange juice and toilet paper and he takes a copy of the Margaret Atwood book he and Jack loved and he drives for three hours up the coast and he sits on a rocky cliff overlooking the beach and he throws the book into the sea. It rises magnificently into the sky, fluttering like a thousand birds in flight, but then it falls quickly and silently and the moment is over before it can feel significant. Carl tries to think about Jack. He remembers looking up from his book to find Jack gazing at him from across the room, his eyes all soft and sparkling like a creep, as if Carl was the most wonderful thing in the world. That look had frightened him, then.

Carl feels his phone vibrate. Tom is calling, again. Carl turns off his phone and puts it back in his pocket. The wind picks up. It stings the skin on his ankles with tiny grains of sand. On the beach below, a young boy splashes in the waves with a Jack Russell terrier. His mother shouts over the barking that a storm is coming in and he needs to get out of the water so they can all go home. The beach will still be here tomorrow.

Aurora's Choice

Aurora was born in the desert. A midnight sandstorm raged around the tent, blew out the candles, sent dirt swirling up from beneath the canvas walls. Grit in the muck of her birth. Grit crusting her soft, just-opened eyes.

The bearded man, robed in black, set a blessing upon her forehead.

Don't worry, little one, he said, this is just the free trial.

She looked up at him with eyes dark as the womb. She could not yet speak his language, but the wordless infinity within her understood. It would be one year. She could survive in the desert for one year.

She started to cry. The bearded man wrapped her in cloth and handed her to her mother.

Until then, he said, with a wink.

The days turned into weeks turned into months. Aurora progressed the way children must progress. She crawled. She giggled. She cried. She gripped her mother's finger with her tiny, straining fist until tears glistened on her mother's cheeks.

She walked at eleven months. She smiled big toothless grins.

She was hungry all the time, but that is to be expected for a child in the desert, especially when the desert is new. Her mother's people did not know how to coax life from this barren soil, how to grow crops when there is no rain. They had known only green rolling hills, little streams and harvests.

Her mother tried to squeeze her breasts dry for Aurora. She pushed at them with both hands. On bad days, there was relief from the big blue-and-white trucks. Grain, milk powder. Enough for another week.

When her first birthday arrived, Aurora could speak a few words. She could cry out for her mother, Mama, and she could say hot whenever she touched things like the metal poles of their tent, or the wheels of the trucks, or the sand, or her mother's skin.

She did not know many words but the bearded man, when he returned, didn't need her to use words. His role was older than language, as old as humanity itself. They would understand each other.

There were two others – twins who had been born on the same day as Aurora in a distant part of the camp. A brother and a sister, green-eyed, dark-skinned. The bearded man seated the three children on the hot earth, propped against a metal trunk in the shade of a peacekeeping truck.

He began his presentation.

I'd like to start by wishing you all a happy first birthday, he said. As you know, today is the day you decide what kind of life you'd like to have. I've put together a few options to take you through, but there are others, so if you feel I've left anything out or there is a particular path you had in mind that you'd like me to include or better explain, just let me know.

The boy seated beside Aurora started gnawing on his fist. Drool coated his hand and ran over his chin where it paused in thick gobs before continuing down his neck.

Option one is to stay put, of course. You can choose to grow up right here, or somewhere just like this, with insufficient food and water, no schooling, the increasing risk of violence and war, severe droughts. It's an unusual choice but it might be for you if you're particularly interested in developing resilience and/or a spiritual practice. Or, I suppose, if you just don't feel like packing up and moving!

He laughed briefly at his own joke but the children did not laugh, so he returned to the solemn, professional demeanour they all expected of him. He produced a photograph of the camp; the children knew the camp well enough from having spent every day of their lives in it, but this was an aerial shot, which gave the area an appealing geometric aspect.

Option two, he said, is to grow up wealthy in a wealthy country. The US is a possibility, or Canada, or even Europe if you have a thing for historical architecture. In this case, you'd be well fed and well educated. You'd be warm in winter and air-conditioned in summer. You'd have a passport that allowed you to travel anywhere in the world without the slightest inconvenience, and it goes without saying you'd have access to excellent healthcare.

It's an attractive option, he continued, pulling from his notes a photograph of a shimmering skyline of glass and steel. Blue sky, blue buildings, a huge body of blue water in the foreground mirroring it all. It looked blissfully cool to the touch, and Aurora immediately pressed the print to her tongue.

The downside, he said, is loneliness and ennui, and perhaps the feeling that life has no meaning because the only things that are valued are consumption and productivity.

The girl beside Aurora scrunched her face into a tight, tortured grimace. She gathered her strength, and then the screaming began. Loud, gasping sobs. Redness fanned out over her cheeks.

Yes, yes, I suppose I can wrap this up, said the bearded man. Just quickly, the third option is some middle-income, middle-class, middling life. This offers the benefit of purpose and striving, while also ensuring you'll have enough to eat, and in many ways it's got the best of both the other alternatives, unless you choose somewhere terribly unequal in which case the crime and violence will mean you spend your life in a constant state of fear. But we can go over the

Gini coefficients of these middle countries if any of you are interested in this route. I'm sure we can find a workaround.

The girl's misery was contagious. Her brother removed his knuckle from his mouth and wailed. They were probably hungry. Aurora herself was very hungry, and the bearded man hadn't thought to bring snacks.

All right, he said, a little flustered, catching a bit of their misery in his cheeks. I was hoping to get to the specifics today, but I see this meeting has gone on longer than you were expecting. It's hot. We all have things to do. Let's pick this up tomorrow and finalise our selections then. You'll need to make a decision by the end of tomorrow so we can arrange flights and asset transfers. Think about it this afternoon and while you're sleeping. Country, lifestyle, family type.

Aurora looked at the three pictures laid out on the mat in front of them. Had the bearded man gone over 'family type'? It didn't matter. She didn't need to think about it. The camp was where her mother was. She tapped on the aerial shot.

Ah, thank you Aurora, you've made my job so much easier. Are you sure? he said.

She nodded, vaguely.

It's a good choice. I must just warn you that if you choose this option, people will use it against you in the future. If you ever try to escape, for example if the war escalates or the drought spreads, they'll say, but she chose to grow up where she did. She made her choice.

But Aurora wasn't listening to the bearded man. She was hungry and inexplicably sad, so she picked herself up on her unsteady legs and tottered off between the tents. It felt like hours since she'd seen her mom.

Quiet as Ants

Julia leaves in February. She packs up her room in the old house with the Oregon pine floors and the pressed ceilings. She sells her desk on the internet. She takes her books to her mother's house and stacks them along the wall in the guest bedroom her mother never uses, the room Julia grew up in. She squeezes all the warm clothes she owns into one red suitcase. 'Come and visit,' she says. 'I think you'd love Berlin.'

Josh leaves in March on an intracompany transfer. 'It's the recession,' he says. 'Big brands are pulling marketing budgets back to their home markets.' The recession was ten years ago, I want to say, but nothing has ever really been the same. He leaves me the gold-painted ceramic Lego man that I love, the one that sat next to the TV in his living room. 'There's a couch for you in New York whenever you want it,' he says.

In April, Lisa moves to France. We go one last time to all her favourite places. The food market downtown that smells of incense and Ethiopian coffee and spiced meat grilled on an open flame. The little circular gallery where sunlight pours in between the vertical wooden slats. The café where she first told me she was falling in love. 'He's French,' she said and I knew that one day she would be gone. We sit beneath the jacarandas and I watch two bees move through the carpet of fallen purple flowers at our feet. A flower falls into my coffee.

'You know, Mark, there's always Skype,' she says. 'We can Skype every Sunday. The time zone's basically the same.'

I smile at her and raise my coffee in a toast. 'To new adventures and long-distance friends.' We can Skype every week. We should. But we won't. I never talk to Freddie or Simone or Nicky and the time zone in London is basically the same, too. So many are in London, or Amsterdam. I see their lives unfold online. Pictures of their holidays in Greece and Turkey. Hiking between the villages of Cinque Terre. Dinner parties in cramped, cosy apartments with central heating. I see the way they form tight new circles of friends with people they barely spoke to at home.

The waiter asks me if I'd like anything to eat. I would like time to stand still, if that's all right with him.

Mbuyiseni leaves in June and so does Siyanda and this time it's different, because everyone expects white people to leave. No one thinks we can tough it out. What does it mean if my black friends are leaving too?

I'm at a house party in Parktown when Princess tells me she's been accepted to grad school in Chicago and I realise it's the same place Tamara left for a year ago. 'You're coming back though?' I ask and she sips her sauvignon blanc, which

86

buys her time, don't think I don't notice that, and she says of course she is. She just wants to have an international experience. They have an excellent academic programme. The opportunity to travel. It was easier, I think, when the people leaving went out in a blaze of insults. This place is going to the dogs, they would shout. It's the next Zimbabwe. It's only homogenous cultures that work, they would say, and at least we knew how to feel about them. Good riddance, we would think, take your negativity and your racism with you. We're going to thrive when you're gone. But Princess?

It's a warm winter afternoon and the air smells of dust. I sit in my garden and watch ants move from a hole in the cracked earth to a crack in the wall beneath my window. It is an orderly procession. One by one, they carry little pieces of something they have broken apart, something I can't identify. How do they know when to follow? I scroll through the contacts on my phone for people to invite over for a drink. There are only acquaintances left, but there is no point in feeling sad about that. There are more acquaintances than there were last week. More than there were the week before. If I put in the effort they can become friends.

I open a news app. Unemployment is up. Schoolchildren can barely read. The president says he'd like his ex-wife to succeed him. The rating agencies say we're junk. But isn't everywhere junk these days? What about Brexit and Trump? What about ISIS?

The grass around me is dead and brown. The whole world is greener than the Highveld in winter, but in summer it comes alive. Heavy rain falls from the sky in surges to thundering applause on the sheet metal rooftops and the sky flashes electric white in the darkness. We can get through this. We have been through much worse than stagnation.

I put the kettle on for tea and watch through the glass as swirls of heat appear in the water. Tiny molecules escape as steam before the water even agitates. Are my friends the steam? Is the country about to boil? Or are we more like moths to a flame, drawn to the bright lights of the world's capitals even when the wilderness is perfectly fine? The metaphor determines the meaning. I look for patterns in everything because no one will tell me what they mean. I take the tea outside and breathe steam into the dry air.

The ants have no answers for me. The rain is late this year.

Across the equator, the shadows fall on the wrong side of the buildings. Are you Australian, they say, are you Dutch? I haven't heard of this university, they say, but we'll keep you in mind for future positions. Do you speak English, they say, what was that word? Oh, we don't do it like that, they say, but it's an interesting way to look at things. But you can't be from there, they say, what about your parents? And their parents? And theirs?

I fly home for Christmas and sit on the hot sand of my favourite beach. A hawker sells granadilla ice lollies and he makes up rhymes as he walks and the ritual is the same as in my childhood, when we came down to the coast for Christmas. The taste is the same too, acidic and sweet, and the seeds crunch between my teeth. The hotel where I stay is brand new. Uninterrupted views over the Atlantic. It's one of countless new hotels in the city since last I was here. They build and build and the rooms fill up with tourists and the restaurants tell you they are full until next month.

The slums are no smaller.

I go for coffee with an old friend. 'It's so good to see you,' he says. 'When are you coming back?' I think of Princess sipping on her sauvignon blanc, Princess who still lives in Chicago, and I say, 'I don't know.'

'I feel like everyone is leaving,' he says and I can't meet his eyes because I don't want to be one of the people who left and I don't want to be the one left behind. I want to rewind to when Joburg was full of friends, not strangers, and jacarandas rained flowers on my street. I want to have people over for lunch on a Sunday and it's not a whole performance to get to know new acquaintances. Small talk and impenetrable smiles.

'I guess it's globalisation,' I say. But it doesn't feel like globalisation, it feels like the end. What is it that ended? We've had no great war. No genocide. No political upheaval for a generation.

'You must get better at Skype,' he says.

'I know,' I say, 'we'll talk more, I promise.'

The homeless woman at the traffic light bangs on my window. She hides her arm in her T-shirt to make it look like it's amputated. I recognise her from the last time I was here, but she doesn't remember me. I hand her some money and she shoves the notes into her pocket and she moves on to the car behind me. I watch in the rear-view mirror how the driver of that car ignores her. He stares fixedly at the road ahead. At me, I suppose. He waits for the traffic light to change.

Always in Motion

He tells her she can call him Trevor. 'Like the comedian,'
he says, which she seems to find very funny. It's partially a
joke – he knows it's ironic; he comes across as serious and
withdrawn – but it's also just easier. Easy to remember.
Easier than telling her anything real about himself.

'You have resting-wise-face,' she declares. She's drunk,
and apparently very proud of her coinage. She sighs theatrically and collapses against the back seat in a heap of blonde
curls. He lets himself feel warm for a second, and relaxed.
Maybe that will be the end of the talking. But then she leans
forward and says, 'Since you're so wise, Trevor, what do you
think I should do about…' and proceeds to tell him all about
her ex, whom she ran into tonight, and was there still chemistry there, because there shouldn't be, they fought so much
when they were together, that's why they had an on-again,
off-again relationship. Trevor feels the pressure build behind his eyes, and it makes him angry – the pressure not
only to listen to this story he isn't interested in but to actually *be* wise and say something thoughtful and uplifting,
because she feels entitled to it and it suits her conception
of him. And why? She will have forgotten all about this con-

versation by the time she sobers up. She won't even remember him. And she isn't nearly as distraught as she thinks she is, either. It's all noise. Drama and empty words.

This is what Trevor's nephew would call 'content' – the stuff that's produced to fill up conversations and social media. He can tell, even with all of her complaining, that she believes things will be fine in the end. And she's right. Things are always fine for people like her.

She doesn't need reassurance, but she wants it. She has that quality that people who have known security in their childhoods exude. An expectation of support. He'd heard her slur-shout her goodbyes at her friends when he picked her up outside the bar in Illovo, and watched her fall into his car like she knew it would catch her. Even if her romance fails, she has her people.

'Where are you from, Trevor?' she asks, when he hasn't said anything in a while.

'No, I live here,' he replies, and she seems satisfied with that.

After he's dropped her off at a block of flats in Killarney, things are quiet for a while. There are no ride requests. He pulls over on a side street near the bridge above the freeway.

He loves these conduits at night. Especially at sunset, in winter, this freeway works better than almost anything else to keep the dread at bay. The city is a living, pulsing thing; it's alive with heavy metals in the blood. Golden headlights flood northwards in the arteries. Taillight embers pull southwards in parallel veins. He can sense the entire vascular system. A deep, steady hum of traffic, of activity, thumping up against the sky, reverberating in his chest.

He is near the heart of the city now. The old diseased, ramshackle, resilient one. The other heart is further north. Marbled, gilded and soulless. What kind of monster has two hearts? All the better to protect him.

It's late now, though. There are almost no cars on the freeway. Just a few long-haul trucks and ride-share drivers. Blood flow has slowed right down. The monster is asleep.

Without all this commotion on the roads, the darkness is frightening. Unless Trevor can move. If he's moving, it means he isn't trapped at home, waiting, listening for when they come for him. In his car, he is invisible. He is free. A tiny speck in the bloodstream. No one knows where he is. No one knows who he is. Even if hijackers come, he has his accelerator. Their attacks aren't personal. It's opportunism, not hatred. They won't hunt him down. If he escapes they'll simply turn their violence on someone else.

The downside of working the late-night trips is that many of his passengers are drunk. Sometimes it's not so bad. They joke and laugh and sing, they tease one another, and he feels buoyed by their spirits, but sometimes they shout at him or demand he find good music and turn it up. They argue with him over a route. Twice, he's had someone vomit, once inside his car, and it took weeks to get the smell out.

Still, he reminds himself: it's better than what he left behind.

His second trip of the night is a couple in their fifties. It's a restaurant pick-up and his couple was the last to leave. Trevor knows this because he watches the waiters stack the chairs on the tables through the restaurant windows as the couple gets into his car. He feels annoyed that the two of them were chased out because they are so obviously still in love, and it's a miracle to see love like this, a bright glittering light in the darkness, and for the restaurant staff to be so unmoved, so impatient, debases the whole thing.

The couple's love is not new. Trevor can see this immediately. They are familiar with one another, comfortable. There is none of the tension of the unexpected between them. But there is no boredom, either; no disdain.

It's too dark in the car for Trevor to see if there are wedding bands on their fingers, but in his rear-view mirror he glimpses the husband – for he wants to imagine he is her husband, this is not an affair, or any kind of relationship with collateral damage – taking the woman's hand. She smiles, softly, and the two of them watch the city rush past from their respective windows.

Trevor imagines their children at home – two boys, maybe teenagers by now, fighting and teasing each other like his brother used to do with him – and he almost asks them if they have children, but he doesn't want to find out that they are childless, that their life is nothing like his dream for them.

He doesn't like to talk too much, anyway, because it's never long before his passengers start to question his own life, and what is there to say that wouldn't leave the taste of metal in his mouth?

He drops the couple off at a home in Parkwood and proceeds to Melville, where he accepts a long ride with a good fare.

At first, he doesn't see the blood on them. The darkness plays tricks on his eyes. Shadows everywhere, cast from the glowing signs of the bars and restaurants. The men position themselves so that the light fails to catch their injuries until it's too late. By the time Trevor realises that blood is seeping from a gash in the one man's forehead, the man is already inside his car and the door is closed.

His friend comes around the vehicle to the other side and Trevor thinks, for a second, that the man is going to drag him out of his seat. That's what happened to that Uber driver in Katlehong, isn't it? They dragged him out of his vehicle, whipped him, destroyed his car, and kidnapped him in their taxi.

Was he ever found?

'You must get out,' Trevor says. 'I can't take you.'

'Relax,' the first passenger says, catching Trevor's eye in the rear-view mirror. 'I won't get blood on anything.' He makes no move to leave.

The second passenger falls into the back seat and he, too, is bleeding. Gashes on his forearms and below his cheekbone.

Trevor's chest has tightened and his own blood is cold. His senses have misfired, again, and reality drains from him. What's left where reality should be is very, very far away.

'What happened to you?'

'This was just an accident. We fell.'

Trevor watches them in the mirror for as long as he can. He is sweating. He needs to know if they were the victims or the aggressors. These are not the wounds of a fall. Why would they lie to him? Are they ashamed of what happened? Humiliated? Or are they the most frightening of all violent men – the kind who smile at you and tell you to relax, who say thank you. The ones with softness around the eyes.

Trevor summons all the strength he has left to push himself back into this world from where he's fallen, that cold, faraway place. He tries to say no, again, to say I can't take you, but the only word that comes out is 'Hospital?'

'We don't need a hospital,' says the less drunk of the two. And then, to placate Trevor, he winks and says, 'Thanks. Just the address I entered on the app.'

'Trev,' the other one says, 'let's go, let's go.'

Trevor puts the car into gear and pulls away. He tries to imagine all that blood as something else, something clean. Soapy water, maybe, or dark, sweet river water. It doesn't work. 'Do you mind if I open the window a little?'

One of them makes a hand gesture that Trevor takes to mean do whatever you like. They are heading west and picking up speed and the open window makes the swirling, thundering air hurt his ears, but it also gets rid of the smell. And it makes their conversation impossible to overhear, which is a relief. No more straining to discern their murmuring – did he understand the language? Did he recognise it? It doesn't matter. He can't hear them. He's set free.

But his body remembers, even if his mind retreats. The adrenaline tingles in his blood. He can still feel it, the memory trapped within each and every cell, the paralysis of being surrounded. The sense of defeat at having run and run and run, and not escaped. The words they used to justify their hatred – foreigner, makwerekwere – were so different from the words they used back home, but the hatred was the same. Thousands of kilometres away and yet here, too, the mob.

When the rock struck his brother, it was as if Trevor felt it in his own body. Then the blood. Pouring from his brother's broken nose, and with the second strike from his eye. Trevor's knees went weak. Was he losing blood? Had he also been struck? For a second, he wanted to be. He wanted to share this with his brother so that his brother didn't have to bear it alone, so that neither of them was alone in this terror.

And then he was hit. On his way down, he thought: why is there so much blood? He thought: all we are is blood. There is so little to hold us in, to keep us from bursting and spilling our insides into the earth. We behave like blood, too. Clotting, sealing shut to heal a wound. It's no different whether it's a mob or your family. An unspoken chain reaction of white blood cells, of people: drive out invaders, knit an impenetrable blockade.

But why do these people perceive a wound, or a foreign object invading? What did he or his brother ever do to injure anybody?

Trevor will do anything, anything, not to think of his brother right now.

They are entering a part of the city that's unfamiliar to him. The small, broken veins of roads far from the organs and arteries. Blood flow is slow, here in the periphery of the great sprawling monster. Clots are easy to form.

He pulls the car over, opens his door, leans out and heaves his insides onto the dirt.

'Are you drunk?' one of the men says from behind him, and Trevor has to laugh. All of these drunk passengers every night and they think he's drunk? He laughs despite the acid all over his lips. Trevor, the comedian.

He wipes his mouth. He gets out of the car, and opens the back door.

'Get out,' he says.

The two men look at him. 'We're not there yet,' says the one with cuts on his arms. He is outraged, but his friend is not.

Trevor knows the expression on the man's face all too well. The friend, the one with the gash on his forehead, is terrified. 'Please,' he says, his voice small. 'Please.'

Trevor closes the door and gets back into the driver's seat.

They could be brothers, now he's had a good look at them. There are similarities. He can't bear to ask them. No one speaks for a long time. He starts the engine. He turns on the sound system. He never listens to his own music when he has passengers, in case they ask him where it's from. But these passengers don't say anything about the music, or the language. They don't say anything at all. No conspiratorial whispering. Nothing to upset Trevor.

Trevor wants to laugh again, and shake himself like a dog after a fight, but he knows how frightening laughter can be. And the fight is only in his cells. They don't even know about it, these two bloodied men in the back of his car. They can't see it.

The two-hearted monster sleeps. Trevor drives the men home.

Little Grey Blazers

Beth found the earrings in Greg's room. In plain view in his white, melamine bookshelf, between his collection of balsa-wood dinosaur figurines and the messy stack of coloured papers, coloured pens and cardboard offcuts that he called his imaginarium. Who taught him that word? Mike claimed he'd never heard it before, but Greg was very definite about his imaginarium. It was not to be tampered with by his parents.

This was the second time she'd found her earrings in his room. The first time, she tried to sound breezy when she asked, what are my earrings doing in here, but Greg blushed anyway, immediately and thoroughly, and said that he just wanted to have a look at them. Was that okay?

Of course, she'd said. Her heart sank. She couldn't help it. She knew she shouldn't feel this way, but her therapist, Alice, had told her that there is no use denying feelings or burying them. They must be confronted to be healed. They must be felt. And anyway, bad thoughts are not the same as bad actions, Alice had told her, there is a distinction. Beth was still a good mother, a good wife, a good *person* even if she allowed herself to feel frustrated or bored or angry at the people she loved or, what was the bad feeling in this case – frightened?

Greg had chosen a particularly garish set of earrings. Cheap costume jewellery. Plastic, it felt like, with a coating of yellow gold and huge red glass rubies. Pendants, clip-ons. If anything in her jewellery drawer screamed drag queen, this was it. How did she even own a pair of earrings like this? She must have bought them for a dress-up party once. She couldn't remember the last time she went to a dress-up party. Maybe one of her brother's Halloween bashes. Before Greg was even born.

That's all Greg was doing – dressing up. It was no big deal.

Beth called her brother. 'What do you think it means if Greg keeps stealing my jewellery?'

'I don't know,' he said. And then, after a pause, 'Are you asking me because I'm gay?'

'Obviously.'

'You know not all gay people wear jewellery, right? You know Vin Diesel is gay?'

'He is not.'

'Well, there are plenty of manly homos. Gus Kenworthy! That Olympic athlete.'

'Oh, fuck off, Jon,' she said. She hung up the phone.

Jon called back immediately. 'Sorry,' he said. 'I didn't know it was actually bothering you.'

'It isn't.'

'Look, I don't think you should read too much into it. How old's Greg? Eight? Don't all eight-year-olds play dress-up?'

'Did you?'

'I think so! But you'd have to ask Mom, I don't really remember.'

'I'm not asking her,' Beth said. Their mother would say something irritating and insensitive. Tell Gregory that they're your things and he's not to take them, she would say, missing the point entirely. Or she'd sigh in that way she does when she tires of Beth walking on eggshells and paralysing herself with the pros and cons of everything, of trying to be so politically correct, as she sees it, and she'd say, tell him not to play with women's things. That kind of conversation was obviously out of the question. When Beth asked for gender-neutral clothes and toys for her baby shower, her mother had said she couldn't find anything like that and, anyway, the whole thing was stupid because they knew it was a boy. It had said so on the scan. She had given Beth almost exclusively blue babygrows, some admittedly very cute tiny t-shirts and hoodies, and a soft toy. (An elephant, which was a cunning choice because it sort of implied masculine qualities without being overt about it, like it would have been if she'd given her a lion.) Greg still loved that elephant plushie, eight years later. He kept it on his bed along with the pink flamingo Beth had bought him to go with it.

Had Beth pushed the issue too far and confused him?

'You know what RuPaul says,' Jon said, 'we're all born naked and the rest is drag.'

'Oh, God.' There was something about earrings that really worried her. If Greg had tried on her necklaces, maybe, or her bangles or even her rings – there were male versions of those things. They were ambiguous. Male surfer types wore those hideous beaded choker things in Durban. They had those chunky rings. But you didn't get surfer pendant earrings. Or did you?

'Beth,' Jon said, his tone suddenly much softer. He had walked somewhere quieter, the boardroom maybe. 'I really don't think this is something you need to worry about. I don't think it means anything. Greg's too young to be thinking about any of this. No one has a sex drive at eight, let alone a sexual identity, right? And anyway, even if he does turn out to be gay, or even trans, you'll be okay with it, won't you?'

It wasn't a test. He didn't ask it as a question. It was rhetorical, meant to put her mind at ease because *of course* she was the kind of mother who was on the right side of progress and modernity and self-expression and raising kids without hang-ups. Of course she would love him no matter what. But trans? It hadn't even crossed her mind.

'Okay, thanks,' she said.

'Don't stress.'

'You'll have to coach me if this becomes a thing. I don't want to say the wrong thing and fuck him up for life.'

'Or fuck *her* up for life.' She could hear the cheeky grin in Jon's voice.

'Too soon.'

'Just don't make a big deal of it, okay? If it's nothing, let it be nothing. And if he's exploring some stuff, let him do that without thinking you'll freak out.'

She decided to leave the earrings on Greg's bookshelf – tidying them away again might make him feel ashamed. She roused their elderly dog, Rosie, from where she was napping in her bed and took her for a walk around the neighbourhood to clear her mind. She searched her podcast library for any episodes about trans kids and found one in *Modern Love*: 'From He to She in First Grade'. Deep breath. She pressed play.

The streets of Parkhurst were quiet after the morning school rush. Beth waved at a gardener hosing a bed of ivy but there were no other people on her walk, no pedestrians, no cars. Just the voice in her ears, kind and soft. It was a beautiful essay. The mother in the story took it all in her stride, made the whole thing sound easy. Their son had liked to wear dresses – Disney princess dresses at first, but then she asked him if he wanted to wear dresses to school and he said yes. She role-played with him, brainstormed how the other children might react so that he was prepared for any insults. The teachers were all very understanding. They said he wasn't the first trans kid they'd had.

In first grade? This was all so American, Beth thought, Americans were streaks ahead when it came to things like this. They just came out and asked you what kind of pronoun you preferred.

Greg's school was a hundred years old, stone buildings and red polished floors and tradition. Little grey blazers, even for the primary school kids. How had she allowed Mike to talk her into a school like that? She hated the idea of single-sex schools, the toxic masculinity, the dysfunctional dynamic it introduced between the sexes. She remembered how much Jon had hated school. He'd never been quite the same since high school – a little quieter, a little less alive. But she'd acquiesced because Greg was only at the primary school, high school was still up for discussion so none of this stuff really mattered yet. Not when they're so young. This school had a good reputation, in spite of how traditional it was, in spite of the single-sex thing, in spite of it being private and privileged and therefore out of touch with the reality of the country. The pupils had seemed happy when she and Mike had gone to see the school for the first time. Happy and confident, and she'd allowed herself to think that that's all that mattered.

But primary school kids could be mean, too. They could be little terrors, blurting out whatever came into their minds without any care for how it might hurt. They could be bullies. That stuff didn't start in high school. Beth thought about Greg's teacher – warm and lovely, but there was no way she'd had trans kids in her class before. She wouldn't even know what trans meant! She'd be totally out of her depth, even with the best intentions. Beth was out of her depth too. She felt like she'd been slipped a drug that bent reality. A parallel existence, the streets around her house so familiar and yet so strange. Was this really the course her ordinary life was going to take?

She would have to fight everyone. Mike, the teachers, the kids, the suburban gossip. Her mother. Jesus, her mother. And how could she protect Greg from any of it?

Would she love him any less?

No, of course she wouldn't. She made herself wait the time it took to feel her reaction. Her genuine reaction. She hadn't denied anything or buried a dreadful dark secret that would fight against repression and come blurting out in some terrible, hurtful way. She would love him just as much. She knew it in her bones. Her therapist would be proud of her for even asking the question, and allowing herself to answer honestly, although now that she had, she felt disloyal and disgusted at herself.

She stepped into the street and almost collided with a bicyclist. 'Watch out!' he called, veering out of her way, wobbling from the sudden change in angle. He lifted a middle finger to her once he steadied. Held it aloft as he disappeared down the tunnel of suburban forest canopy. Maybe it wouldn't be so bad if Greg didn't grow into a man.

When Beth picked Greg up from school he was the same as when she'd dropped him off. It seemed impossible after the morning she'd had.

'How was your day?' she said, catching his bright green eyes in the rear-view mirror.

He was breathless with enthusiasm as he told her about the T-rex he was making in pottery class and how Vuyo had said it looked so lifelike it would be too scary to take home. Rosie would be scared and would run away, so he was going to store it in the art class at school and Beth would have to come see it there.

'That's fine,' she said, smiling at his reflection. 'Just tell me when it's ready and I'll come in. You don't think I'll be too scared?'

'It's just pottery, Mom,' he said, rolling his eyes. 'It can't hurt you.'

She decided her brother was right. She would let it be, for now, say nothing. Let Greg take his time. She wouldn't tell Mike about the earrings. She wouldn't even tell her therapist. They would both have opinions and expect her to have opinions but really, she didn't. She was emptied of all opinion. The only thing she could do was be there for Greg and make him feel loved, no matter how he grew up. One day at a time.

On the morning of Beth's birthday, ten days later, Greg burst into her bedroom at 06:43 even though she had given him strict instructions to wait until 07:00.

'What is it?' she said, fumbling for her glasses on the bedside table. 'Is everything all right?'

'Happy birthday, Mom!' he shouted. He presented Beth with a mass of green and pink paper, artlessly taped together with masking tape. 'Open it,' he said.

She peeled apart the misshapen package and found within it a necklace made of cardboard cut-outs strung along a piece of string. Each of the cards was cut in the shape of the earrings, forming pendants with borders coloured in gold pen. A bright red hexagon of coloured paper was glued to the centre of each golden shape.

'Do you like it?' he said. 'I made it to go with your earrings.'

Beth pulled him into the bed and gave him the tightest hug. 'I love it,' she said. His hair smelt of apple shampoo and that intoxicating scent he had, warmth and sleep and love. Maybe all children smelt like this until their hormones came along to ruin it.

'I knew you would,' he said, laughing and trying to extract himself from her vice-like grip. 'Do I know you or what?'

Going Home

Nothing. For about the tenth time in as many minutes, Nick leant back into the couch, yanked his phone out from the front pocket of his jeans, and checked for messages. Irritating, compulsive behaviour. A month in New York and already he missed home. He should be out exploring the city. He should be meeting new people, having new experiences, not moping about in his apartment, tied to his phone with apron strings. Of course there'd be no messages. It was nearly 19:00, which meant it was well after midnight in South Africa. So much for the global village. Time zones, the last great heretics against an ever-compressing world of technology and instant gratification, demanded he be present in his new American life.

Most days Nick was happy with the distance. He got to text his friends in the mornings and, by late afternoon, when they were heading to bed on the other side of the world, he was in his stride, confident and relieved to experience the city without having to report back on it. The novelty of it all exhilarated him.

But exhilaration is exhausting. He can't keep it up, not every day. Lying on the couch, flipping between vapid reality shows on TV, half-reading the news on his laptop and consulting his phone, Nick was tired of feeling foreign. He just wanted to hear someone who sounded like he did, who wasn't putting on an accent. He wanted someone who found him funny. Back home, people found him funny.

He'd run into Dustin on the subway the other day and Dustin seemed happy to see him. They hadn't seen each other in, what, fifteen years? Not since primary school. Dustin had said 'We should get together sometime,' which was a classic thing to say in those situations, whether you meant it or not. But Dustin had seemed to mean it.

It wasn't hard to find him online. They had loads of friends in common. He smiled as he started up a message. Weird to be messaging Dustin, of all people.

Great running into you on the train the other day, Nick began, scanning through Dustin's pictures. Dustin looked so different from the shy, kinda femme kid Nick vaguely remembered from school. He was hot now, and well built, although he was often at black tie galas and gallery openings so there was a risk he was the kind of douchey expat who made up for feeling provincial by acting all posh and pretentious.

At least he was coloured – biracial, they'd call it here? Or just black? – so he probably wasn't a racist asshole. That was the other kind of person you risked running into among South African expats. The white ones, anyway. *You're looking great. New York agrees with you.*

The message showed up as read. Did Dustin have nothing better to do on a Wednesday night than check his DMs? Nick wrapped up: *At any rate, I thought it could be good to grab a drink sometime. Let me know when you're free.* They hadn't really been friends when they were kids and Nick felt good about reaching out to him now. Dustin was probably lonely and homesick in the big city.

Sure, came the immediate response. *Shall we get that drink tonight?*

Nick checked the time for an excuse. Too early to pretend the night was over, but meeting up now required all the effort of showering, changing, being charming in real life. He just wanted to hang out on the couch, maybe send some texts with the vague promise of company in the future. He walked to the window. The street below was full of people in a silent movie – walking and laughing together, walking and talking seriously into their phones, regaling one another as they sat at the outside tables of the bar opposite. Nick couldn't hear a thing. Their lives were silenced by the double-glazing of the windows and the deep drone of air-conditioning units.

The bar Dustin had chosen was a warm, quiet spot in Chelsea with exposed red brick walls and the kind of dark leather booths that make it feel like everything is going to be all right. Deep, rich hues and masculine lines were counterbalanced with small tables and close, intimate spaces, somewhere between a gentleman's library and a cuddle.

111

Dustin had done well: Nick liked it. It was a good choice, also, because it reminded Nick of Cape Town. If he ignored the accents of the bar staff and pretended the beer in his hand tasted like Black Label, he could be in any of the bars on Bree Street.

'I've been here three years this month,' Dustin said. He'd been telling Nick the story of how he ended up in finance. It sounded senior, although Nick knew corporate Americans loved to call everyone a vice president. Maybe looking Dustin up had been a mistake. He definitely had a bit of that pretentious twang Nick was worried about, enunciating his words as if Queen Victoria had been personally involved in his education. He seemed so smug about how well he knew the city, too, laughing when Nick let slip he hadn't heard of whatever restaurant he was talking about. Dude doesn't have to prove anything to me, Nick thought, fighting the urge to roll his eyes. Dustin's gestures were also a little camp. He crossed his legs like a girl. Nick tried not to let it grate him – he remembered it had at school – because Dustin really had grown into an incredibly good-looking guy, even more so than the pictures had let on. His scrawny frame had filled out. His biceps made the sleeves of his turquoise t-shirt tight when he moved them, and his chest stuck out just enough to cast a shadow.

So Nick tried the expat thing. It was what he was there for, wasn't it? To create a little bubble in which they were the insiders? Us against the world. 'What's up with Fahrenheit?' he said. 'I was trying to bitch about the heat in the subway the other day, to this insanely sweaty woman who was standing next to me. Bright red. I say to her, "Jesus, it must be forty degrees down here," and she looks at me like I'm simple. I looked it up later and forty degrees isn't even hot in Fahrenheit.'

'Yeah. I guess it's strange not to use the metric system.'

This wasn't working. They were talking about units of measurement, for Christ's sake. Maybe being from the same country wasn't enough to force a connection, to ease the homesickness. Nick would have left already – he'd drunk the requisite drink and stayed for a polite half-hour, and Dustin was like a fucking dead fish with his conversation skills – but a strange sexual chemistry was keeping him there. Strange because Dustin was dull, obviously, and so gay. The whole effeminate thing really pissed Nick off. Could these guys not just be normal men? Did they have to go around pretending all the time? But there was also something seductive about Dustin. Maybe because he was coloured. Nick had never slept with a coloured guy before and had always wanted to. The brown of their skin was so beautiful, like a deep tan after a summer in Plett. He loved their cheekbones and their blunt, direct attitude. He loved the idea of crossing that divide. Dustin had dimples, too. Nick had a thing for dimples.

Nick locked eyes with Dustin in the way that always got him laid. 'Are you seeing anyone at the moment?' he said.

Dustin smiled. 'I'm not,' he said. He looked down at his hands and tapped the table. Then he got up to get them both more drinks. Nick watched him. Dustin's movements became so much more relaxed as he got to the bar. He stood with the comfortable slouch of someone talking to a friend, and laughed easily when the barman made some joke that Nick couldn't hear. Why was Dustin so aloof and uptight with Nick – did he think he was being sophisticated?

'I can't believe you're single,' Nick went on when Dustin sat down again and handed him another beer. Dustin tilted his head in acknowledgement of the compliment but wouldn't take the bait. Nick powered on: 'I see you like macho okes,' he said, 'proper rugger buggers.' As soon as he'd said it, he knew he'd overplayed his hand. Was he trying to get a rise out of Dustin? Was he flirting? If it was the latter, he was normally so much better at this. It was pretty cringe to reveal he'd been going through Dustin's photos online, trying to figure out if any of those guys were his boyfriend. He sounded creepy and overly familiar because Dustin was giving him nothing, just sitting there like a condescending blob. Why should Nick have to work so hard to get the conversation flowing?

Dustin shifted in his seat. His face was impossible to read. Finally, he broke Nick's humiliating silence. 'Are you still in touch with anyone from school?'

'Ja, I still see a lot of those guys,' Nick said. This was better. He could do some reminiscing with Dustin. 'Remember

Chris?' he said. 'He shared a digs with me at varsity. And I'm good mates with Gugu and Thabo. Remember them?'

'Of course I remember them.'

'What about you, man? You keep up with any of the guys?' Nick couldn't remember who Dustin used to hang out with. He was one of those quiet kids who never really made an impression. 'It's funny, I don't think we really saw much of each other at school. We were in Maths together. And soccer, I think.'

'I didn't play soccer.'

Nick laughed. 'Oh, right.' He remembered now. Dustin hadn't played sport. His parents probably couldn't afford the gear.

'I didn't enjoy school much, Nick.' Dustin took a sip of his whiskey and stared at the glass in his hand. He wanted to say something else, Nick could see. He was burning up wanting to say it. Nick waited. The silence was less uncomfortable this time. It was almost a relief to see Dustin looking hesitant, instead of pretending he was better than him.

Nick wanted to lean over the table and kiss him, but Dustin was so closed off. This was the trouble with introverts. You could never tell what they were thinking. Dustin might reject his advance. He felt his cheeks flush.

'Right,' Nick said at last. 'I get that. It makes sense.' He didn't want to be playing therapist. If Dustin couldn't tell him what was on his mind, maybe that was for the best. No awkwardness. No unnecessary emotion. He leant back and ran his fingers through his hair. 'I loved school, you know. But it's not for everyone.'

Dustin laughed, Nick had no idea why, he must have thought of something funny in his head, and after that point Dustin was so much more relaxed. His movements became more organic and less controlled, and with each new story he was warming to Nick's sense of humour. The more Dustin laughed at Nick's jokes, the more Nick liked him. Maybe they could be friends, after all. It was nice to know someone from home. Even better when the guy from home was this handsome.

When it was quite a bit later, Dustin sighed and said, 'Well, since I'm going to be hungover at work tomorrow anyway, would you like to come home with me?' Nick grinned. He was adrift in warm colours and background chatter. Yes, he said, he would very much like to do that.

'I hear this area's super gay,' Nick said, punching Dustin on the shoulder and stumbling a little. 'Don't be such a cliché, man.'

Dustin was taking a ridiculous amount of time to find his keys. 'Don't worry, *man*,' he said, drawing out the word like it was from a foreign language, 'no one's asking you to live here. Your record is clean.'

Nick was suitably berated. He was being loud and obnoxious. He had drunk too much at the bar. He counted the stairs in his head as he climbed. A simple, mechanical task would restore his equilibrium.

Dustin's space was surprisingly beautiful. Old wooden floors, working fireplace. Expensive art on the walls. Dustin had clearly made a lot of money since coming to America. He had unexpectedly good taste.

Dustin poured them each a glass of red wine. He passed the bottle to Nick. 'A little taste of home,' he said, winking and raising his glass. Nick's eyes filled with tears when he read the label – it was hands down his favourite wine in the world. How did Dustin know?

He placed the bottle on the counter, wiped his eyes with the palm of his hand and grabbed hold of Dustin's head. He pulled Dustin into a kiss. Dustin's tongue barely moved in his mouth. It kept to itself like a servant at an extravagant party. Nick could see he would have to take control here. He bit Dustin's lip, pushed him against the red brick wall, and ripped off his t-shirt. Dustin's abs cascaded in undulations of maple syrup and shadow. A trail of soft black hair beckoned. He put his hand into Dustin's pants. Soft. He rubbed for a second or two. Nothing. It all made sense. Dustin was clearly a bottom. He didn't want to be admired. He wanted to be told what to do.

Nick unzipped his own jeans and stepped out of them. Rock hard and ready to be serviced. He put his arms up behind his head and waited for Dustin to kneel. Nick's smirk always worked on guys like Dustin, guys who needed direction and force. The arrogance got them off, did something to them that Nick would never understand. Dustin hesitated.

But then slowly he got down on his knees. He looked up at Nick. He had the strangest expression in his dark eyes. It wasn't lust. He began to kiss and suck. It had worked. Guys like Dustin just needed to know who was in control. Nick moaned and shoved Dustin's head down all the way onto his cock. Dustin struggled against him. Half-choking, he pulled back against Nick's hand. He gagged, and wiped his mouth with his wrist.

'I can't do this.'

'Of course you can,' Nick said, forcing Dustin's head back down.

'Get the fuck off me!' Dustin roared. He staggered to his feet.

Nick stepped back. 'Sorry, sorry,' he mumbled, lifting his hands in a gesture of truce.

'Who the fuck do you think you are?'

Nick tried to laugh. 'It's what you invited me up here for, isn't it?'

'You think it's funny? You think it's okay to treat me like that again?'

'I thought you were into it. Sorry dude, my bad.' Nick looked around for his underpants. Was this over? Should he pull them back on or— 'Wait,' he said, 'what do you mean "again"?'

'Oh, fuck off.'

'Seriously Dustin, what are you talking about?'

'You're kidding. You don't remember?'

'Remember *what*?'

'Oh, this is great. I spent years in therapy trying to work through all of this and you've forgotten all about it. You and that prick Thabo, you know, the one you're still "such good mates with",' his face twisted into an ugly expression as he made the air quotes, 'you tormented me all the time.'

'Oh, come on man, we were kidding. We were kids!' It had all been harmless, hadn't it? Why did Dustin have to take everything so personally?

'You called me a fag. Shoved my face in the dirt.'

Surely Nick hadn't been so rough. 'I'm sure—'

'You made me kiss your dicks and say how much I loved doing it or you'd tell the whole school I was a fag.'

Nick's mouth fell open. Dustin had crossed his arms over his chest and was kneading his biceps compulsively as he spoke. He stared fixedly at the floor and in that gesture Nick could see him as he had been at school. The same small, frightened boy, on his knees in the dirt behind the music room. His muscles didn't look so big or impressive any more.

'You even pissed in my mouth, you fuck.'

Nick felt like he'd been punched in the solar plexus. How could he forget something like this? How could he have done it? Coldness spread through his blood. He could see eleven-year-old Dustin crying in front of him, streaks of clean skin on his dust-covered cheeks.

'What the hell is wrong with you, Dustin? Why did you go down on me then?'

'I don't fucking know. I thought it would be cathartic or something.'

'To blow me?'

'I wasn't planning to do that. Or inviting you up here. I don't know, it just kind of happened. I thought we'd gotten past it at drinks. I thought maybe I could prove to myself I'd let it go. Personal growth or something.' He looked up at the ceiling and let out a short, humourless chuckle. 'I thought the whole reason you contacted me was for some kind of atonement. You were so complimentary, kept going on about how good I look. I thought it was your way of apologising.'

Nick couldn't look at him any more. He wanted to shut these memories away. Lock them up again wherever they had been, deep in the recesses of his mind, but they wouldn't yield to his force. An unrecognisable shadow person was intruding on his golden-boy childhood, possessing his body, using it to push other kids around. Had he really tormented people like that? Laughed at their weakness. Hated them for the traits he hated in himself. Anger and fear rose up in his throat again, knotted together, forgotten and so familiar. It was difficult to breathe.

Dustin slumped down on the kitchen floor. His lips looked raw and his eyes were red. '*You* looked *me* up,' he said. 'I thought shame, this guy has nothing going on at the moment, he's lonely and needs a friend. I cancelled my plans tonight. I figured here's my chance to be the bigger person: forgive and forget. I assumed you'd have become a nicer person by now. Especially when I realised you're gay.'

Nick sat down too. 'I'm not a bad person, Dustin,' he said.

Dustin looked him straight in the eyes. 'I don't care if you think you're a bad person or not. Whatever stupid story you tell yourself to make yourself the hero. You fucked up my life. I want you to know that, if you didn't before. You're an asshole.'

'Oh, come on, you're okay. Your life's turned out pretty well.'

Dustin said nothing after that. The clock on the oven said 02:00, then ten past two, and still no words seemed like they could fix it. After another minute, Dustin rolled his head back, closed his eyes. 'I think you should leave.'

When Nick didn't move, Dustin got to his feet. 'Now,' he said.

Nick stood and buttoned his shirt. He gathered his things from Dustin's sleek granite countertop. Phone, keys, wallet. Dustin opened the front door. Nick hesitated at the threshold. He couldn't leave it like this. What could he say? He stuck out his hand. Dustin looked at it.

'Look, Dustin,' he said, trying sound casual, light, 'I know I'm not—'

'You don't know what you are,' Dustin said. He closed the door in Nick's face.

Nick stepped down the stairs in a daze. The lights in the stairwell shone so brightly his eyes ached. The streets of New

York were deserted. Drunks shuffled about in their own little worlds. His phone vibrated in his pocket. It would be Dustin saying goodbye. He needed it to be Dustin saying goodbye so that he could feel normal. Feel like himself. It was a flurry of messages from South Africa coming in. Six hours ahead on a Thursday, his friends were either arriving at work or firing off messages while stuck in traffic on their way to it.

You have fun last night? his sister asked. *What did you get up to? Have you made any friends yet?*

We're missing you, buddy! Thabo said. *But I hope you're having a blast over there. I'm gonna look at flights to come over in December. It's been too long, man!*

Nick turned off his phone. His featureless reflection looked back at him in the black, empty screen. He descended slowly into the subway. The air that had been trapped in there all night was damp and unbelievably hot for 02:30. He was sweating like a marathon runner by the time he got to his platform. A group of drunk students swayed, laughed and gossiped loudly about a friend they had seen earlier on. 'Come on!' one of them groaned. 'How long is this train going to take? I need AC. It must be a hundred degrees down here!'

Kingdom of Prophets

To my right, far below: white beaches, the Atlantic Ocean. To my left: the steep slopes and undulating peaks of the western face of the range. The contour path is busy on a sunny day like this, too warm for the season, but I can't think about climate change right now, not today. I hold my breath as I overtake other hikers, as joggers move past me, aerosolised particles swirling from their lungs into mine.

When the pandemic started, I thought it was the perfect metaphor for our modern culture. Like anxiety itself: tight chest, shortness of breath, isolation. It was the manifestation in our bodies of our late-capitalist psychic disease.

I can't find the poetry in this trauma any more.

Mom was so breathless on the phone this morning I could barely hear her. She was tired after five minutes, and I had to end the call to let her rest. Five minutes is the same as yesterday, I remind myself, no worse. The hospital will take care of her. They're monitoring her blood oxygen levels, her breathing. I'll speak to you tonight, Mom, I said. I love you.

I was shaking when I hung up the phone. I wanted to call my brother, but we'd only make each other worse. He's also trapped on the other side of the country in a province with closed borders. Roadblocks on the freeways. We can't get to her. We can't do anything but call and worry, and send stupid messages with heart emojis, telling her we're sending white light and healing energy, the universe will protect her. The kinds of things I don't believe but they feel good to say. Better than nothing, anyway. They bring her comfort.

I do not breathe as I run past a group of hikers who aren't wearing masks. My chest burns. It screams at me to pull down the breath-damp cotton from my mouth and gulp in the air, but the air's contaminated. I fight it. I make it to the last copse of umbrella pines on the contour path. Usually I would stop here. There's a stone bench in the shade facing the ocean. I love the view, and these old trees – ruddy trunks fissured like winter lips, roots tentacled through the earth. Today, I don't stop. I turn off the crowded path and up, onto one of the trails that zigzags towards the cliffs. It's quieter on these steeper trails. Deserted. I take a full, deep-chested breath, and begin my ascent.

These mountains are the only thing that calms me. A stillness that comes from their immensity and almost infinite age. Nothing we do or say matters much in the face of this wall of rock, formed millions of years ago by the break-up of Gondwana, the rupturing away of South America, Antarctica. The mountains were once so enormous that the high plateau I aim for, the iconic flat top that towers over the city, was once the sediment at the bottom of a valley, among the lowest points in a range that has eroded away. From above, the peninsula is a river delta of rock. It grows wider as it meanders north, collapsing and subsiding in parts, before falling into the city. To the south is a steep, narrow point ravaged by storms.

I climb for an hour and stop to rest on an outcrop of rock. Like magic that works only if you believe in it, the dull green uniformity of the fynbos will not shatter unless I pay attention. It's a flat smudge of colour on the mountains, except no two bushes are alike. No part is the colour of the whole. The silver tree catches my eye first. The fine hairs on its leathery, feathery leaves reflect sunlight like silk. In the shadow of the boulder beneath me, deep orange cobra lilies rise from snake-tongued leaves. Pink and white oxalis constellations on the earth. And that strange, sharp plant with its vivid purple flowers and leaves like emerald shards of glass. I have never found the name for it. The apps on my phone suggest all the wrong matches. Out of the blur comes impossible specificity. Leaves as fine as pencil shavings. Leaves as fat as spatulas.

And all around me, the kings of this tiny, dazzling kingdom, the proteas.

They are born in fire and I like to think I can see fire in their inflorescences. The explosive shapes, the colours of burnt orange and hot red and phosphorus yellow. Styles that shoot from the flower heads like sparks from fireworks. They are the phoenixes of the natural world. When wildfires blacken the sky with smoke and parts of the city need to be evacuated, the proteas burn along with everything else, but in those flames their seed pods explode. The seeds scatter into the wind.

The trauma passes from generation to generation, unbroken.

I've always loved them. Maybe because you don't find them growing wild anywhere else on earth. Maybe because they're so unusual, so prehistoric-looking, with their geometric shapes and their woody, resilient foliage. Flowers without fuss or fragility. Flowers, but make it masc.

They are named after Proteus, the shapeshifting Greek god. He was also a prophet. He knew the answer to every question you could ask. He knew when you would die, how a war would end, whether a woman was ever to love you, but he tried to keep his secrets to himself. To get an answer, you needed to catch him by surprise, tie him up with rope and wait. He would transform in order to escape – becoming fish or python or boar – but eventually he would tire and give you the answer you sought. These blooms all around me are named for the thousands of different forms they take, but I like to think they are prophets, too. We've tied them up with concrete, tortured them with heat and broken the pattern of their rains. Now we wait for the prophets to answer.

Is this pandemic the first plague of many?

Will we survive what we have done to this planet?

I trace the hard bracts of a dusty pink inflorescence with my fingers. My mind isn't helping. My mind brings me back again and again to the dread I so desperately need to escape. I need to be in my body, not my thoughts. I need to move. To feel the repetitive pounding of my feet on the earth, my lungs expanding and contracting, my heart beating in my ears.

I set off again towards a kloof in the peaks above me. The wind picks up. It cools the sweat on my arms and neck. It funnels wisps of mist up from the ocean behind me. The condensation pours over me like a river rushing against the laws of gravity, and billows over the crest of the range, white and soft.

I am alone on the path, tucked between sheer walls of rock. Before Mom was hospitalised, I would have been too afraid to come up here alone, scared of falling and twisting an ankle, scared of being attacked by one of the muggers you hear about who hide on these trails, far from where anyone can hear you scream. I feel nothing but relief to be alone right now, away from the news and the virus. Away from people.

It's steep in this last part of the ascent. I break often to catch my breath. The proteas here, in the cold and wind, are shorter than their cousins on the sunnier slopes, but they hold on. The yellow-white ones are in bloom right now, bulbous buds like ostrich egg shells among paddle-shaped leaves. Last month's pink inflorescences hang scraggly on their branches, fibrous and dishevelled.

In *Landmarks*, Robert Macfarlane writes about the need for a 'particularising language' for the landscapes we love. The way light strikes water just so, the distinction between moor and bog. We protect only what we love, and the more we name and notice about the natural world around us the more we love it. I think of all the names I don't know, and the names that have brought me no closer to love. Maybe it's that English evolved on the other side of the planet, in a different climate with different references. Common English names for our indigenous species say more about the trans-planted Europeans who settled here than about what they were seeing. The names invariably reference something *else* – wild olive, wild almond. The Latin names resist affec-tion. I wish I knew the indigenous names the way Macfarlane quotes Gaelic and Scots, but the first peoples here were driv-en off, assimilated and exterminated. So many languages and names, all the folklore and connotations that were woven into them, have been lost.

I have the particularised language for my mother. She's not a generic patient, a statistic in the daily pandemic reports. She's the sixty-eight-year-old woman whose left eye closes slightly more than the right one when she's laughing so hard she's crying. The woman who stresses the first syllable of "harass" instead of the second. She hovers by the living room door when we watch scary movies, pacing and cover-ing her eyes and telling us she's never doing this again. She thinks Joni Mitchell is the only musician who can make her feel anything. She's the salt-and-pepper-haired, sun-mottled eldest daughter of five, grandmother of one, the woman who buys me the most thoughtful spontaneous gifts, who drove me to school every day of my childhood and cheered for me when I said I wanted to be the first boy to take another boy to my high school dance.

Now she's in that bare hospital bed with oxygen pressed to her mouth. Do they try to make her feel less alone? Will they hold her hand? Squeeze her shoulder? Can she even see their faces through all of that protective gear?

I climb until I reach the high plateau. Rock gives way to white sand, grasses and brush. A few steps from the edge and there's no evidence of the city all around me. This is almost untouched wilderness up here, entirely indifferent to my presence. It's this indifference that I crave.

I walk towards the reservoir. It's full again; the rains have been good this winter. The dark water laps at the top of the stone wall. It's the colour of rooibos tea, a fynbos tincture. My eyes prickle at the sight of so much water. The drought has broken, for now. The drought that made international headlines, made us famous as the canary in the coal mine for climate change. I remember the clock counting down the days until the taps ran dry. The army was being readied, government said, to keep the peace.

I watch sunlight dance on the ripples. We have another year. Another chance.

There's an inscription in the stone I've not noticed before. The reservoir's named for a British governor. When this was another country, a dominion. From the word "dominate". It's all connected in my mind – the drought, the pandemic, the poverty in the streets of Cape Town. The homeless men and women who rifle through my rubbish every Tuesday, then knock on my window and ask me for food. It all comes back to that one hideous impulse of the strong over the weak, the colonists, the capitalists, the church, ISIS, the alt-right. Dominion over others. Dominion over the earth.

I head towards the deep ravine that runs through the centre of this plateau like an axe wound. Restricted access, you need a permit to enter, but there's no one up here to stop me.

It's steep and narrow, this chasm chiselled out by water, and it takes me down into a lush cocoon, even further away from people and stone walls and cities. There's a microclimate in here, a hidden pocket of Afromontane forest. Every sound is amplified – the birdsong, the wind rustling the leaves. The shift in vegetation is so sudden I'm disorientated, fallen into a land of pixies and sprites. There are no proteas now, no familiar shrubs and grasses. This is real forest, the kind that's rare in this country. Huge trees and ferns and moss. I'm surprised to feel anxious when I lose sight of the stone reservoir wall above me, the last thing anchoring me to the world of humans. I wanted to be alone and I have done it. But instead of feeling relief I wonder why this is restricted access. What is in here that I'm not supposed to see?

The footpath clings to the left of the ravine. To my right, a precipitous fall into tangled branches. Somewhere beneath those branches – I can't see it, but I can hear it – the tea-coloured rushing water. If I fell, there'd be no space for a helicopter to rescue me. Luminous, back-lit vegetation droops over my head, cascades over the steep slope of slick, black mud. Spanish moss on the trees, like a haunted Louisiana bayou. But these aren't bayou trees, they're yellowwoods, and pock ironwoods, and milkwoods. The trees of the Tsitsikamma rainforest, of the overgrown sandy paths to the beach on childhood holidays. This forest once spread from here to Ethiopia, they think, a lush belt of giggling streams and ancient trees and monkeys and orchids. Now, a few pockets hang on in the wet ravines, the cooler mountain ranges.

I met the man who told me all this a few years ago in another small pocket of forest, two hours' drive east of Cape Town. Some of the milkwoods in that forest are a thousand years old, he said, but most of the young ones don't survive – there isn't enough rainfall any more to make it through the canopy to the seedlings. Instead, when an old tree falls, it sends up new trunks where it fell. You can think of the milkwoods here, he said, as one organism. One very old milkwood that moves slowly over the land, rising again from where it rests in the sand.

I like the resilience of that. And the velocity. The pace of continental drift, not ambulances.

My mind returns again and again to loss, but I'm not listening. Loss is not the language being spoken here. Something always survives even if it is not both mother and child. These peaks will erode into the sea, but it is the work of aeons. The crags don't worry. The trees let the wind tickle their leaves without thinking about the future. The great wildernesses of the world will be okay. They'll shake us off and start again, after our deforestation and emissions, after we've destroyed ourselves and our food supplies and poisoned the seas and unleashed plagues and storms. The forests retreat, but they find places to hide. The fynbos hangs on in hot, deficient soil, rising again and again from wildfires and drought. For millions of years this kingdom has been burning and growing. Falling and starting anew. Creeping across the earth to find water.

This, right now, is all that exists.

The rocks are slippery with life. The river rushes. The canopy is thick and deep and nameless and perfect.

My phone vibrates in my pocket, startling me. My brother's name is on the screen. We spoke yesterday. There's only one reason he'd be calling again so soon. I find a place to sit among the ferns and I take a deep breath.

Hello?

Three Readings

Dude, where are you? The reading starts in, like, five minutes and they won't let you in if you're late. Where? Oh okay, yeah, that's not far. No, it's the opposite corner. Red neon sign. Hurry up. You've gotta see this: there's this crazy old woman here in a tight, full-body, purple velvet tracksuit. She must be eighty in the shade. No, I promise you. Massive rings on every finger, earrings the size of baseballs. I know, right? Grandma thinks she's Kanye. What? Okay cool. Five minutes. I'm in the back. See you soon.

*

Oh Carol, I don't care. I think she looks fabulous. She doesn't give a fuck. Don't you just love New York? There's every kind of person here. Wall Street bankers. Frat boys. Hipsters. Grungy little Brooklynites with tattoos everywhere. Drag queens. No one's judging. No one cares. Makes a nice change from Indiana. Yes, it *is* that bad – have you forgotten? People would be staring if this were Indiana. They would. And you know what, good for her. Whatever this look is, she's nailing it. Yes, I was also thinking she must be Russian. Russian or Ukrainian, something like that. Those Eastern Europeans love a bit of velvet and bling. What do they call all that kind of jewellery? Rocks? No, that's not what I'm saying. Never mind. What do you want to drink? I think I'll just go for a white wine.

*

I adore the readings on Thursday nights, I come every week. Every week I'm here, never miss it. They're usually no good, but that doesn't matter so much. It's better than what everyone else my age is doing. Sitting around watching TV. Waiting to die. Neglected by their families, abandoned by their dreams. No thank you, honey! You can keep it. Give me bars and art and bright young minds! This is what it's all about. Creative expression. Bravery. Let me tell you, it takes bravery to commit a story to writing. And then to share that story with a room full of strangers? I wish I had that kind of chutzpah. My stories stay in my head. They go round and round, round and round like a Ferris wheel, they never stop, they never leave me alone, like I'm possessed. Sometimes I think I won't die until I've told the stories I need to tell. I can't die. The universe won't allow it. It wouldn't be right.

I've got amazing stories, let me tell you. Real stories. I don't even have to make it up. Everyone writes the same things now. The same crap. It's all formulas, beats in the same place, hooks. That's why AI can do it, that's why they're all freaking out about AI. And even when these writers try to sound different, when they try to be quirky and original and unexpected, they still end up sounding just the same because they're trying to be different in the same way. And what they do is they drift further and further from reality, from what it feels like to live inside a life. Meet-cutes in movies, now, they're ridiculous. First dates. Does anyone really go to a shooting range for a first date? Or meet during a bank robbery? Of course they don't. But writers don't want their story to sound just like the next one. But what about the human experience? This is all style over content. Minimalism. Maximalism. Magical realism. Bullshit! But I salute you, kids! I salute your bravery. You're out there and you're creating art and it's fucking fantastic because you don't care about the odds, the machines that are coming for us, the economy that doesn't value artistic expression, or maybe you do but you create all the same, and most of us will never follow our dreams. We'll be 'getting around to it' until we die.

I'm not saying young people don't have anything to say. I didn't say that. Some of the best writers that ever lived were young when they lit up the world. Plenty of them were rich and privileged too, so you can keep that other popular half-assed theory to yourself, the one about needing to have *lived* to write. Lived with that godawful earnestness as if only debauched or impoverished living counts as living, counts

135

as inspiration for real art. Tolstoy was an aristocrat. I've been both debauched and poor and I don't have a book deal, do I? I'm not reading from my 'upcoming collection' at an artsy dive bar in the East Village, am I?

I do think it's sad, though, how so many fascinating people blaze through life without leaving a trace. Wise people, funny people. They entertain, they electrify, and then, *bam*, they're gone. Lights out! Like they never existed. A handful of people remember them, maybe, for a while. Tell their anecdotes at cocktail parties, but there's no lasting impression on the world, you know. No real contribution to the way we all think. Their friends were changed, but is that enough? It didn't spread. It didn't *go viral*. And those are the lucky ones. Plenty of us don't even influence our friends. They don't think about us at all. Our inner life doesn't make it out of our mouths. Trapped in there like our mouths are stuffed with rags. So here we are, with inferiors writing stories every day, churning them out in movies and books and shitty TV shows that glue people to the screens like zombies. They're everywhere but are they any good? Is anyone even paying attention? Does it matter, one way or the other? Let me not get maudlin. These bright young things get it done. They create the canon and people read it and they love it because that's all there is. You can't mourn what never was, can you? You can't miss what you only imagined. I can't judge, baby. I'm just a spectator. What have I written? A few lousy notes in the margins of life, that's what.

These young people are trying, they're trying! And that's what it's all about. I love it. I just love it.

*

The MC steps up to the podium and waits the polite amount of time for the patrons to notice that she's standing there. She doesn't clink her glass or tap the mic, but the crowd does settle down. She thanks those in attendance for coming, reminds them that it's their presence that makes evenings like this a success. She points out the restrooms and introduces the first reader, a Brett from Long Island City.

Brett stands with the practised nonchalance of an introvert who is waging a quiet war against his introversion and hates that writers are expected to perform in front of live audiences but understands the importance of projecting a confident brand, because people are brands in the information-saturated, attention-deficient world of 21st century late-capitalism. He clears his throat and leans forward and begins reading.

His voice is soft and warm and it contrasts in an unexpected and delightful way with his story, which is neither soft nor warm and is in fact a story about bullying and this leaves the audience wondering whether a) Brett has turned his own painful experiences into art or b) he has a dark imagination with hidden depths or c) he doesn't understand himself at all and still needs to find his authentic 'voice' and, if c, who does he think he's kidding? The excerpt that Brett reads is not long enough to indicate whether the narrator is also the protagonist but one or both of them is a nasty teenage girl who catches her younger brother masturbating and mocks him relentlessly in front of his first girlfriend and then takes him to the movies as if nothing has happened and some in the audience are struck by the way the younger brother forgives and forgets and how this so beautifully captures the archetypal resilience and playfulness of sibling relationships in youth, while others in the audience harbour suspicions that the younger brother actually feels deeply resentful in a way that is not clear in this particular excerpt but that will come to destroy his relationship with his sister later on in the book. Brett has allowed minimal access to the interiority of his characters and those who notice such things conclude that this ambiguity is what gives the story its animating tension.

The eccentric old woman in the front row lifts her Manhattan skywards, spilling a little on her purple velvet sleeve, and shouts out a whoop of encouragement as Brett smiles and walks back to his seat, vulnerable and exposed. The audience applauds. A small glowing mass of energy arises near the place where Brett had stood at the podium. About the size of an apple. Perfectly spherical. It radiates pure white light but swarms with little purple ribbons of luminescence like those close-up pictures of solar flares that you sometimes see online and trust because they come from reputable-sounding websites. It hovers there, a magnificent cosmic body stripped of its mass and immense proportions and relegated to a bar in the East Village. It does not emit heat. It quivers a little, or our perception of it does. It defies the laws of gravity. No one in the audience comments on its appearance.

*

At first I wanted to write a story about coming to New York and finding myself, but I suppose everyone wants to write that story, don't they? It's been done. A dreadful cliché now. Small-town gal arrives in the big city and thinks her experience is interesting. Well, I was no different. Thought my life would make for a good story. Pretty scandalous. But I missed the moment. Now there are immigrants from much more interesting places than where I'm from. You've got your Syrians, your Rwandans. Trans women from Venezuela, for Christ's sake.

I knew some amazing people in those early years in New York, just after I got here. Amazing people, you wouldn't believe, from my time as a stripper. Talent and personality up the wazoo. I could name names but you wouldn't believe me. You'd think I'm making it all up. I know what you're thinking, anyway. You're thinking you see my jewellery and my velour and you know me already and you know my story and I'm just some old blonde bimbo with no brains and no one to tell me I'm too old to dress like this. First off, this blonde's from a bottle, honey, and I'm plenty smart and, second of all, strippers don't deserve their bad rap. We have brains. There's no reason to believe we can't have brains. And even us old ones, we're still people. I wasn't the only one at the club who read books. I've read more books than anyone here tonight. I've read all the greats. People think if you don't go to college you can't enjoy literature, or have ideas, but that's just classist bullshit right there. Back when I still worked the clubs I'd get to bed around 05:00, sleep till 10:00 and then lay in bed all morning reading. Till 14:00 or 15:00 some days.

Holly also used to read. She would take the *New Yorker* with her on the subway, but she hid it in her bag when she got to the club because she didn't want anyone thinking she was too smart to have fun. She was a lot of fun, believe me, but she could also tell you who was winning in the primaries and how it would change your life and what the Vietnam War meant for liberation movements in Africa, too.

Holly and I got a private gig in The Hamptons once. Some rich guy saw us at the club and asked if we did private parties and we said yes even though we'd never done a private party in our lives. The whole thing turned out to be pretty vanilla anyway, nothing to be frightened of, but before we knew it we were spending almost every weekend in The Hamptons giving lap dances and handjobs to the richest men on Wall Street while their wives watched the kids and bored each other with stories about their little darling's school concerts by the pool. Holly's was the first vagina I ever tasted. We went down on each other at these parties. I'd never done it before and it made me feel sick that first time, but it also made me feel giddy when I thought about how my mom back home would take the news. The attention was fun. The men cheered like we were their favourite sports team and sometimes they sprayed champagne all over us like their team had won.

*

The MC walks back onstage to introduce the second writer. She ducks her head to avoid the glowing white star, which seems to be growing, and it flashes and swirls, angry like the lightning heart of an enormous electrical storm. Most members of the audience continue to ignore this heavenly body. They must think: it can't be real. It's the wrong size and anyway, wouldn't they feel its gravity and heat? But the old woman in the front row stares fixedly at it. She wonders if it is a metaphor for something.

The second writer is introduced in a jovial way that makes the man sitting in the second row, three seats from the left, next to the two businesswomen with matching black purses and the wide, wholesome faces of Midwesterners, think about how relieved he is that he no longer works in advertising. He remembers briefing voice-over artists to sound

just like this. To speak as if they were on the verge of crack-
ing up with laughter no matter what they were saying
because it makes audiences more receptive to the message.
Talk about yoghurt as if it's hilarious. Isn't short-term insur-
ance just the funniest thing? He despairs briefly for human-
kind's susceptibility to formulas like this, being tricked into
paying attention and trusting whoever's speaking. He wonders if this suggestibility is a common characteristic of all
social species and if, by extension, his dog back in his apartment is cheered by particular tonal qualities in his speech.
He aches with deep horror, for an instant and not for the
first time today, when he thinks about how marketing tac-
tics have penetrated every aspect of modern life from how
we talk to one another and present ourselves as brands to
how we dream. We are at the start of this terrifying experi-
ment in mass manipulation. We thought the peak was 1950s
advertising when you could say whatever you liked in an ad,
doctors recommend this cigarette, for example, but really
we're at the beginning, it's all getting so much more powerful and sophisticated, the machine learning preying on our
weaknesses and blind spots, and you see it already in elec-
tion results and political polarisation and soon we won't even
know what's real any more, whether anything we see is real,
and when he thinks about giving up our sense of reality to
this hive-mind that maybe even the malevolent billionaire
tech class who fund it don't fully understand, and when he
thinks about what this means for the future of democracy

and humanity, he feels a bit sick. Can a straight line be drawn from advertising to this nightmarish world of individualised, monetised senses of reality? He tells himself he can escape this trap because he's not so online any more and anyway he shouldn't feel responsible for it, because no cog is responsible for the whole system. It was fun work, sometimes, meaningful, and he no longer does it. This emotional journey takes no more than ten seconds. There's more than enough time for this ex-advertising man to refocus his attention on the MC and catch the tail-end of her introduction of the next writer in that jocular way he can't stand.

The second writer, Neil, is another man, thirty-two, who grew up in the East Village. The MC says this makes Neil a local, as if local means anything any more, as if specificity and community and context weren't the first lambs to be sacrificed on the altar of globalised cultural production. He's about five foot ten, with grey eyes and hair that looks perfectly arranged to affect a carefree attitude to life.

He opens his book, his first to be published and the recipient of numerous awards. He reads a passage from two-fifths of the way into the story, where a lonely college student who may or may not be the central character realises that he no longer loves his gay lover but continues dating him out of pity and out of the guilt he feels for having encouraged the lover to come out of the closet in a religious town where his parents were influential. The audience applauds loudly and there are a few shrieks of support from a group of people sitting together towards the back of the room, presumably friends of the author or gay people who are particularly delighted to witness another example of queer life being mainstreamed into literature.

The two women with matching purses nod appreciatively as if they know a thing or two about living in religious small towns. The college student who arrived late checks his phone for news from his friends who haven't yet confirmed where they are meeting for drinks after the readings. The old woman in the front row is likewise too preoccupied to clap. She stares at the purple-white star and wonders if it is a representation of her life. The star grows. It looks particularly menacing after a third Manhattan.

*

I got into porn my second summer in New York. I guess most people don't think it's a big leap from stripping to porn, but strippers aren't as slutty as everyone thinks. It is a big leap. But we chose to do it. It wasn't some tragic manifestation of coercive economics. I thought it would be fun – and Holly and I were already sleeping together for show so how different would it be? When Holly and I chatted about it she said it would be a feminist statement. It affirmed the power of our sexuality and our right to choose what we did with our bodies and our lives. We'd make good money and shag a bunch of hotties, too.

It turns out the men in porn aren't hotties. At least they weren't in those days, in straight porn. At first I thought it might be because men weren't scrutinised in the same way as women by the culture, they were allowed to exist beyond their looks, and have a rich life evaluated on more esoteric or cerebral terms, but the more movies I was in the more I came to think that maybe viewers preferred the men to be totally average-looking so that they could imagine it was them, they – the viewers – were the real stars. It affirmed their masculinity. If the actors were too handsome then maybe viewers might feel gay for getting off while watching them, or they'd feel ashamed and inferior by comparison. It ruined the fantasy. Seeing cocks was fine. They could imagine the cock was their own, especially if the cock was huge – they all liked to imagine they had a huge cock, the obvious contrast between the porn star and the viewer at home didn't seem to be off-putting in that case, they were immune to the comparison – but they didn't want to see a face if it wasn't our face and it didn't have a finger or a cock inside it. They wanted to watch us, and that was kind of exhilarating. Knowing all these people out there were fantasising about me, dreaming about touching me, wishing I was real. No one wants to watch me now. No one even looks at me now. They look away. Try not to stare.

My second idea for a book came from that period. I couldn't write about coming to New York and ending up a stripper, but how many people had read about feminist porn stars who discussed philosophy and mingled with CEOs? Holly thought it was a great idea. She was going to help me write it, she had such a beautiful way with words, you could listen to her for hours. She died, then. Taken by Aids, which she must have got from the men we were sleeping with. She was the only person who knew about that part of my life, who knew me, who could help me do it. She phrased things so beautifully. She was funny and thoughtful. I didn't see the point after that. Ended up not writing that book either.

*

Chris! Check, she's crying. I'm telling you, dude, she's crying. No, it's not laughter. Watch the breathing. It's different. She's crying and she's talking to herself. Okay, don't stare. No, I know it's sad, but I mean. Awkward. Keep it together, grandma! Cry at home like the rest of us! Right? Reckon that last reading touched a nerve? Maybe she's a big ol' lesbian. Totally! Yeah, the way she's holding her drink, for sure. Pretty butch energy. Although, velvet? I dunno, man. It doesn't add up. Haha, no that's not cool. Rapper raccoon? Because of all the smudged mascara? Too far, dude. Too far.

*

The MC walks back onto the stage, for the last time tonight, she says. She is more relaxed now, with fluid movements and a voice that sounds less like a radio spot and more like a human after a few drinks, a human that has come to the end of performing an act that she was anxious about performing and that seems to have been well received. The audience has grown progressively louder during the readings and the chatter takes a while to die down after the MC begins speaking. She thanks everyone for coming and starts off a self-congratulatory round of applause for keeping literature alive in the age of instant digital gratification.

The MC gives the podium a wide berth on her way back down to her seat because the purple-white star is almost as big as a man now and she seems unwilling to either touch the star or acknowledge its presence. Is it giving off a faint hissing sound? No one can be sure.

The choice for a final reader has not betrayed the historical moment. It is a woman, at last. She is tall and slender with wild, black, ringleted hair like an Egyptian. She clears her throat and reads from the opening of her novel. In it, a quiet woman from Idaho moves to the big city and becomes a dancer. The premise triggers a brief moment of irritation in a number of the listeners who believe they have heard this story a million times before – isn't it the plot of *Coyote Ugly*? – but they recover and they allow some emotional experience to break through because what the opening lacks in originality it makes up for in the quality of its prose. The language is simple but lyrical, the pacing is good, the mood is optimistic and enchanting. The audience decides that they like the young woman from Idaho. They are rooting for her.

The young woman in the story fumbles through odd jobs, trying to survive by waiting tables and working at a bodega. She gets fired from both and ends up in the last place she ever imagined herself: knocking at the grungy back door of a strip club, that week's *New Yorker* poking out from the top of her threadbare handbag, waiting to speak to the owner about a job.

This last story gets the loudest applause. It is impossible to tell if the audience considers it the most nuanced and relatable of the three stories or if the writer's face and sex and racial ambiguity give the moment a feeling of historical triumph. The applause may well be because of the lateness of the hour: most members of the audience are drunk and feeling expansive. The servers have not stopped moving since the readings began, filling glasses with three shades of wine and pouring beers. The writer smiles widely at the audience, increasingly certain that she got the tone just right. She laughs at the third round of cheers because laughter is, for a certain kind of person, the only possible reaction to having your work validated by a room full of strangers.

The purple-white star shakes and hisses but neither the readers, nor the MC, nor the audience pay it any attention. They are not going to let a burning ball of gas ruin their good time. The old woman at the front mutters under her breath, talking to herself, one imagines, since no one else is listening to her. Her voice grows loud enough to pierce the collective hum of the crowd only when she begins to curse and so those who start paying attention to her agitation are suddenly put off, their pity souring to disdain. She's a drunken mess. A potty mouth. The woman stands and throws her Manhattan – her fifth of the evening – at the star. It splashes on the restless surface without drama, more of a damp plop than the crackling fireworks sound one would expect. Is the star her life? If it pops, will she die? Will she be given that moment? The moment where people rush over to her, fuss over her dead body, call 911, breathe into her mouth, wonder who they should call? Will they discover that she had no family, that the only person who ever loved her died nearly forty years ago? Will they regret not hearing her stories? Will they finally look her in the face and notice the colour of her eyes? Hold her in the centre of their attention?

The star does not explode. It shudders gently and begins to deflate. The light goes out first at its edges. It gets smaller and smaller until it is the size of a fist, then a pea, then a little purple pinprick hovering in the space-time continuum.

It is gone.

The old lady sits back down in her chair. She looks at her wrinkled, sunspot-pocked hands for a longer period of time than most people would spend on such an activity. She orders herself another Manhattan. One of the men who read from his story earlier tonight looks at her briefly while she talks to the barman. He thinks: I could use a character like that.

The Witch

It had been raining for so long that the leaves on the forest floor no longer crunched. Sodden and soft, they absorbed Hanret's footsteps into their quietness. Gently rotting undergrowth. Mycelium networks and silent, scuttling invertebrates. Hanret placed her bare foot lightly between twigs and ferns. Stepped slowly towards her prey. Eyes glanced up. It could only hear soft drizzle. The cool breeze moving between ancient yellowwoods carried the sound of Hanret's breathing away.

She raised her weapon slowly. Shifting shadows of trees. Shhhhh, said the rain.

Suddenly, movement. A spear, hurtling. The warthog looked up. Alert, suddenly afraid. Electricity fired from its brain to its legs – run! – but the signal was not fast enough, did not reach the muscles in time. Squeals of agony. A sound unbearably like a baby's cry. Hanret pulled herself from the shadows and ran to the dying animal. She had missed the heart, her spear was in its stomach. It kicked and screamed. Eyes wide, lids pulled back. Its nostrils flared as it looked right at her. Did it know what was coming? Could it see the abyss? It could not beg. Could not plead. A consciousness, a whole world of experiences and yearnings, trapped in a skull, behind a mouth that could not speak. A clumsy, uncoordinated tongue that rendered it wordless. Hanret slapped her own cheek. It was cruel to falter. She ripped the spear from the hog's stomach and slashed its throat. She sat and held the animal against her body as it shivered. Sang an old folk song from her childhood to ease its passage, or maybe to calm herself down. She wept when the light had gone from its eyes. The rain soaked through her faded, torn dress, blurring the blood like a watercolour painting. She wiped her eyes and turned the hog over. It was a male and it was an adult. She had not killed a mother. She had not killed a child.

The grief subsided over time. She prayed to God for forgiveness and to the spirit of the animal. She thanked the forest for her sustenance.

Sun broke through the clouds at last. A soft white glittering on the leaves of the canopy. She began to drag the dead animal back to her dwelling. It was slow, heavy work. She broke often to rest and to sip from rain-filled arum lilies.

By afternoon she was home. She was starting to think of it as a home now, this sorry excuse for a structure. Branches and torn strips of cloth. She had assembled the skeleton on her third day in the forest. It had been hot that day, no rain, and she had lain down beneath the mossy, lichen-covered trusses and fallen asleep with nothing but the distant forest canopy as her roof. In the weeks that followed she layered fern leaves and bark and bits of an old dress and plastered it all together with mud. A roof that slanted down to become walls, like the huts she had seen before on the outskirts of Jan's farm. It was enough to protect her from the forest, though it was not the forest she needed protection from. It was Jan.

The day Hanret finally fled the farm had not seen the worst of the beatings. When Jan was really angry, when the brandy was sour on his breath and he cried while he beat her – on those days, after those attacks, she could not flee. She could not walk from the kitchen to the bedroom without collaps-ing. Her legs gave in, her groin throbbed and bled, bruises spreading like mould on old cheese. Always, he kicked her in the groin. You barren bitch, he would sob, are we going to die alone on this farm?

We're not alone, Jan, she said. We have each other.

That would soften his anger a little. A moment's reprieve. And then it would harden, again.

What's it all for, he raged, without a legacy?

She wanted to say to him that it was like this for every-one, that children could not prevent the cruel passage of time and inevitable oblivion. Did they remember their own great-grandparents? The legacies they had built? Of course they didn't. They knew nothing about them. The only thing that matters is what we do right now, she wanted to say, but she kept her mouth shut and she waited for his fist. It came in harder after a moment of vulnerability.

On the day Hanret fled, Jan had slapped her only once. It was morning and he was in a good mood. She made him eggs and toast and even diced up the last of the ham and put it into his eggs because she knew how much he loved ham, and she sat beside him while he ate. She must have looked bored then, or at least distracted, not entirely focused on him, because he turned to her and said, no matter how well you cook, a woman with no children is no woman at all.

She packed up her things after breakfast. Two dresses – one lilac and one white – a spare pair of shoes, a hair comb, a ball of yarn and a knife blade, all rolled up in a sheet and tied in a knot. She snuck out of the back door while Jan was walking his fields. She made it to the edge of the forest by early afternoon. Pushed deeper into the wilderness as the sun began to fall. Jan's farm was at the very edge of the colony. The last outpost of the known world. He would have to go back to come forward, retreat to the other farms to gather a search party, lose days moving in the opposite direction.

She walked for three days before she stopped to build shelter. She was deep in the forest by then, too far for the dogs to sniff her out, for the farmers and their whips and belts and their ideas about what a woman should be. There was a stream nearby. Emerald ferns unfurled around her and trees so tall they tickled the sun. This was a place of magic where maybe, at last, she could find some peace.

Hanret lifted the warthog onto a fallen tree trunk to get it out of the mud. She took her spear and pushed the blade between its ribs. The flesh was tough. It resisted. She pushed the blade deep, then drew it down between two ribs, split the chest in two. She tried to get leverage beneath the sternum but the bones would not crack. She leant on the spear with all her weight. The shaft – the branch she had bound to her knife to make the spear – snapped.

It had been days since she ate. Her last meal had been a few measly mushrooms foraged from the undergrowth. She was too weak to butcher an animal. She had no idea what she was doing.

She retracted the broken spear and used the knife to slice off bits of soft flesh. The hog's cheeks. The belly. The penis. The eyes.

Blood all over her hands and her dress. Blood on her cheek. Running along the bark of the fallen tree. Hanret was shaking and dizzy. She felt a deep, despairing ache within her bones, for the necessity of violence. For the impossibility of living without harming others. Nausea welled up in her throat but beneath it, further inside her, was a hunger that would not subside.

Flint. Sparks. Damp kindling eventually coaxed into flame.

Hanret skewered the tender parts of her warthog on sticks, roasted them above the fire. The hair scuttled inwards, melted, bright red glowing fibres and then smoke. The pink flesh bubbled and browned, a life desecrated into meat. Hanret devoured each of the pieces as soon as it was cool enough not to burn her hands. She kicked dirt and wet leaves over the fire. She could not risk the light. She crawled into the dark cavity of her home and fell asleep.

She woke before dawn to the sound of voices. Whispers, very close. Her heart thundered. There was no way out of her shelter but through the front, where the voices were. They would surround her and overpower her. Drag her back to the farm to cook and clean and provide for a husband who despised her. A man who saw her as nothing but a defective womb.

The voices spoke again. Was it . . . were they children? Hanret held her breath. They were children's voices. Speaking the language of clicks.

What are you doing here? she croaked as she clambered out of her hiding place.

The children froze. They turned to face her. Two of them. A boy and a girl. Siblings? No older than nine. Smooth, frightened faces. The ochre skin of the people of the forest. They were both dressed in animal hides. They had been standing over Hanret's hog, but they stepped aside now. The animal was even more of a mess than she had left it in. Gore and bone. Exposed chunks of flesh. The children must have knives on them. Hanret moved slowly. Lifted her hands as she approached. The boy looked down at the ground. His sister hissed something at him and he removed, from behind his back, a severed leg. He placed the bloodied limb close to the carcass.

Are you hungry? Hanret asked.

The children watched her.

She moved her hands to make eating motions in the air. Her eyes pointed towards the dead animal. The boy shook his head quickly. The girl nodded.

Can you help me cut it? Hanret asked.

They remained completely still.

Hanret mimed stabbing the air. Pulled the imaginary animal to pieces. She pointed again at the hog and then at herself and then at the boy. His sister was transfixed. He looked up at Hanret and nodded.

It did not take long for the boy to butcher the animal. He was strong for his age and his people were excellent hunters. Hanret helped in the beginning, but it became clear she was getting in the way. Instead she built a fire with the girl and observed, as she built it, how the boy separated joints, where he placed the blade, which angles worked best to crack open bones. She had not paid attention when Jan tried to show her things, but this she needed to learn. If she were going to survive another three months in this forest, or live here until she was old, she would need to get better at killing, at breaking, at subduing the parts of her that hated all of this.

They roasted the hog in pieces. They ate in silence. The boy and girl looked at the fire. Hanret tried not to stare at them. Their faces were so beautiful and so very sad. Had they lost their parents? Had there been another colonial war? There were rumours among the farmers of a famine inland.

Do you want some more? Hanret asked. She handed each of the children another chunk of meat. The corners of the little girl's mouth lifted slightly. There was a look of Hanret's mother in the girl's face. The same large, melancholy eyes. The same sharp nose. If Hanret had been able to make children, she liked to think they would look like this. A different skin, of course, but the same gentle temperament, the same soul.

Hanret, she said, pressing her blood-soaked hands to her chest.

The children did not respond, so she did it again. Hanret. The girl jolted upright. She understood. She touched her own shoulder and offered a name. The boy did the same. Hanret tried to replicate all the clicks with her tongue and the children laughed and, for the rest of the meal, their silence was softer at its edges.

The children stayed. The first night, they slept outside, but on the second night it rained and they followed Hanret into her cave of leaves. The floor was wide enough for three people to sleep but only if they pushed themselves close to one another. Hanret fell asleep on her back with the little girl beside her. The boy fell asleep on his side watching the two of them. Hanret dreamt of the dogs. They came for her in the shelter, sniffed her out from the scent of her clothes. She could feel their warm, damp breath. Smell the meat and blood. Their teeth snapped at her from the entrance to her haven, snarling like demons, as if she hadn't been the one to care for them, feed them and stroke them and throw little sticks for them to fetch when they were puppies. Behind the dogs, in the distance but getting nearer, she could hear Jan's voice. Come out, come out wherever you are. She stood up to run but the dogs overpowered her. Knocked her back to the ground and tore into her stomach. Strips of flesh and muscle came away in their teeth. Her womb. They were eating her womb and she knew – she *knew* – that there was a baby in there. They ripped at her and she screamed and thrashed and her shoulders were shaking and she opened her eyes and the little boy was shaking her. The girl was watching with wide eyes. The boy stroked the hair out of Hanret's eyes. She was crying, but she didn't know if it was from the dream or the boy. He lay back down on the ground and went to sleep.

The next morning, they set a trap. The boy taught her how to catch animals with rope and leaves. They caught a hare and ate it. They caught a baby bushbuck but Hanret let it go. No babies, she said to the children, but they did not understand. They foraged for mushrooms and medicinal plants. The girl showed Hanret which leaves to use for cuts and which to use for stomach pains. Hanret began hanging leaves and roots to dry from the branches of her shelter and, on the fourth day, she and the girl made potions.

After a week, the children were fatter. Fuller cheeks when they smiled. Stronger muscles on their arms. Hanret wrapped her fingers around the boy's bicep and he laughed shyly and pulled away. She squeezed the girl's cheek between her fingers and pretended to eat it, so plump and juicy. She could feel the flesh between her own abdominals and her skin when she knelt to start a fire. Meat clung to the bones of her upper arm where once there had been nothing.

She taught the children a few words of her language and they taught her a few words of theirs, but most of their communication was wordless. A hand to the mouth to eat. Two hands to the side of the head to sleep. Eyes for use as pointers. There was no need for hello or goodbye because they never left each other's sight. The children were the first thing Hanret saw when she opened her eyes in the morning and she found that with every passing day, the sight of them brought her more comfort than the day before. She no longer slept on her back. She no longer feared every bark or rustling of leaves. She lay on her side and held them close to her chest and the boy, at last, no longer felt the need to watch her.

It was the girl who tried one morning to communicate something Hanret did not understand. Hanret had not yet learnt the words the girl was saying, but she could tell it was something important. The girl stood in front of the shelter and moved her arms back and forth. She pointed to her brother, agitated. She raised her hands above her head. Her brother began to speak rapidly to the girl and he leapt to his feet and the two of them spoke quickly and then the boy, too, joined the charade. Running motions. Hands above their heads. A hand to the ear.

Hanret listened. She could hear nothing but the wind. Had they heard an elephant approaching? The boy made a gesture that looked like a trumpet, but what was the fuss? They could stay out of the way. Elephants charged only when provoked.

The children started walking. Hanret shook her head, no, we don't need to leave, but they didn't listen. She grabbed the boy's hand but he shook it loose. He pointed for her to sit.

She followed them between the ferns and trees. We don't need to go, she said, over and over. We are safe where we are, no one can see us, but the children did not listen. They climbed up through the undergrowth towards the crest of a small hill. They were moving quickly now. Hanret tripped on a root and fell and they did not wait for her. She ran after them, something deep and black building in her chest. Where were they going? At the top of the hill, the girl stopped and turned around. She pointed back towards Hanret's home. Go, she seemed to be saying. Go.

What had Hanret done wrong?

The girl opened her arms. She hugged Hanret, a tight, long squeeze, then let her go. She and her brother started down the other side of the hill. They did not want Hanret to follow. Only then did Hanret see it. A glimpse of ochre between the trees. Deep in the next valley there were people. People of the forest. It was not elephants the children had heard. It was their parents.

Hanret grabbed the girl and hugged her again. She pulled her close and wrapped her arms around her and squeezed. Tears streamed down her cheeks and onto the girl's shoulder and she let out a noise she did not recognise. The hug was too long, she knew, too tight. She was frightening the girl but she couldn't stop. She couldn't let go. The girl struggled to get away but she was trapped. The boy pulled Hanret's arms off his sister and pushed Hanret to the ground.

They left without saying another word. She watched their small, nimble bodies move quickly between the leaves, disappear behind a tree, reappear briefly, merge with the shadows.

There was no evidence of the children back at her shelter. Nothing to say they had been there at all. Dried blood and bones where they had butchered their kills. Medicinal potions in gourds lined up on the floor. Healing potions – for cuts and bruises and stomach ache and fever – but there was a word for medicine women living in the forest, and it made Hanret feel cold. The potions had been the little girl's idea, hadn't they? Had she dreamt the whole thing? Had the forest made her lose her mind?

A woman with no children is no woman at all, Jan had said.

Maybe Hanret was something else.

Why Don't South Africans
Read Fiction?

'Why don't South Africans read fiction?' Greg says. He presses his fists into his eyes and groans theatrically so Thapelo
knows he's joking, sort of. He already regrets saying it.
Generalisations are so evidently untrue (not *all* South Africans, obviously), but how can he speak without generalising?
How can anyone? Words are only ever partially accurate.
If you look for trends, if you comment on anything, you are
ignoring the caveats, the nuances and exceptions. He mutes
the radio. Of course, he can't say he doesn't like the song
that's playing right now because maybe he only *thinks* he
dislikes the song for reasons of musical taste when in fact
he dislikes it because the lyrics are in a language he doesn't
understand (isiZulu), and the style hails from a musical tradition that is alien to him, and so really it's about the culture
of the singer, Greg's restricted access to the lives of the
oppressed, his complicity in propping up the system he in-
herited? How can he ever know?

It's impossible to speak his mind with this muck of history on everything. It stinks and it stains and it weighs us
down. He speaks to avoid suffocating in it but he knows these

outbursts are blunt and inaccurate. Myopic at best and toxic at worst. 'I know not enough people read anything,' he continues, already backtracking, qualifying, anticipating Thapelo's response, 'and the education system is broken and books are expensive. I know. But fiction sales are disproportionately dismal. When people read, they read sports biographies, cookbooks, political exposés. If Siya Kolisi writes a memoir, or that guy from Eskom, people read it. But if I write a story?'

'People read memes,' Thapelo says. He winks at Greg and smiles his beautiful, crooked smile. 'It's going to be fine, babe, stop stressing. The market's small but it's growing. Becoming more relevant with every great new black author who comes along.'

'If I wrote in Afrikaans I'd be sorted. Afrikaans readers are much more patriotic. They're loyal to local authors.'

'Because there are no international Afrikaans authors for them to disloyally read.'

Greg offers a convincing smile. Must Thapelo split an infinitive to make that joke? And must everything be a joke? This is his problem too. The longer Greg makes no money from his writing, the longer he is a financial burden on Thapelo. An unlikely addition to Thapelo's black tax. Thapelo's advocate salary is good but how many dinners in Nelson Mandela Square can he afford to pick up for the two of them without growing resentful? Thapelo wants to pay for Greg. He offers. But he must think it's weird, surely?

'You know what it is,' Greg says, 'we have an empathy problem. As a nation. We can't imagine what it's like to be someone else. We don't want to imagine it. A white tannie in the suburbs doesn't want to go through the experience of being unemployed and black. And the unemployed black man doesn't want to know that a tannie in the suburbs can also feel heartbroken or hopeless. We're so brainwashed into defending our positions that we can't inhabit each other's humanity.'

'Mmhmm.'

'One of our many scars from apartheid.'

'Ya.'

'Everyone's so angry because anger is easier than empathy.'

'Or maybe,' Thapelo says, his tone very different from just a minute ago, 'we're angry because half our young people can't find work. Because we're the most unequal country on earth. We have bigger problems than novels, Greg. And incidentally, how many books are published in isiZulu or Setswana? Our writers are the problem, not our readers.'

That's actually a publishing issue, Greg wants to say, but he leaves it. He says nothing. Lets the verbal slap sting. He read a book about gay shame only last week and it said that defensiveness is a sign that someone feels invalidated and that gay people are hypersensitive to invalidation because they have endured so much of it in their childhoods. Thapelo must feel attacked. He interprets so much of what Greg says as an attack.

Greg takes a slow, steadying breath. He gets up, walks behind the armchair that Thapelo is sitting in, a mid-century armchair of teak and navy blue velvet, and he rubs Thapelo's shoulders. '*You* have an empathy problem,' he says. Thapelo jerks his head around but when he sees Greg sticking out his tongue at him, he relaxes. Puts his hand on Greg's hand. Should it really be this difficult to talk to someone you love?

*

Thapelo gets back from Botswana late on a Thursday afternoon. The flight is bumpy because it's the Highveld and it's summer and though the pilot tries to fly around the worst of the thunderstorms, the sky is stacked with dense titanic clouds that close off any escape. He orders another beer before they begin the descent and the flight attendant looks at him like he might have a drinking problem. Or like she thinks this is so bloody typical of the entitled black middle class. After the aggression of her eyebrows, the beer does nothing to calm his nerves.

He spends the train ride in to Sandton feeling happy to be alive and a little surprised. The world is brighter and cleared of its haze, even in the dark tunnels beneath the city. The stations glow with the light of a xenon sun and there are details everywhere. Brushed, golden scalene triangle earrings hang from the earlobes of that dark, beautiful woman in the pencil skirt. A tiny sticker of Africa flashes past on the noise-cancelling headphones of a grungy teenage boy. Witty lines jump out from the ads on the sides of the station walls. Wealth everywhere, and opportunity, and the kinds of people he would never have seen as a child. Never have known they existed, if they did. He can make things work with Greg. Everyone goes through rough patches. All relationships sometimes feel like misunderstandings.

'Happy birthday, old man,' he says to Ofentse as he gets to the bar in Parkhurst. He hugs his friend and smacks him on the shoulder and pulls up a chair on the opposite side of the table. Joyce scoots up to make room between herself and Greg. Thapelo leans over and kisses Greg quickly on the lips.

'How was the trip?'

'Fine,' he says and he doesn't think his tone is hostile but Greg looks hurt by the brevity, as he always does when he gets a one-word response to a question, and so Thapelo says, 'I think we're going to win the case.'

A cheer erupts around them. Half-empty pint glasses raised towards Thapelo. 'Thanks,' he says, 'thank you,' and then he looks around the table for a different conversation to join so he doesn't feel so exposed. He leans in, tries to figure out what Joyce and Keke are talking about. Something to do with financial modelling. He raises his eyebrows. Orders a Soweto Gold.

Greg isn't talking to anyone. He's blushing a bit and staring into space, not looking anywhere in particular. 'You'll love this,' Thapelo says, quieter this time so no one else can hear. 'The advocate I was working with in Bots told me South Africans are very boring because we're so obsessed with race.'

Greg's expression freezes. He's trying to work out whether to enjoy the sentiment or find it problematic. The next thing he'll say will be to ask if the speaker was black. The predictability of this interaction already makes Thapelo tired.

'Was he black?' Greg asks.

'She was a she. But yes.'

Greg relaxes. He doesn't have to launch into a tirade about the insensitivity of his fellow white folk. He doesn't have to prove that he is not one of *those* white people who thinks black people should just get over apartheid. Thapelo used to love this about Greg. Now he finds it tedious. He wishes he hadn't brought it up.

'It must be nice to live somewhere it doesn't matter,' Greg says.

Thapelo's beer arrives. He takes a sip. Leans in to the group conversation. Greg hesitates, then puts his hand on Thapelo's knee. Thapelo watches him out of the corner of his eye.

'Don't do that,' he says, 'don't look so proud of yourself for being the only white guy here.'

He meant it as a joke, but it didn't sound like a joke. The light goes out of Greg's eyes.

The phone vibrates in Thapelo's pocket. His brother is calling. 'Thapelo,' he says, 'Mom was attacked again. I think you should come home.'

*

The drive out to Rustenburg is long and tense. The roads are bad. The landscape is dry and hot. Dust in the air. Small plots by the side of the road where families live out their whole lives without anyone knowing. Thapelo is restless behind the wheel. He barely speaks. Greg tries to be quiet too. He knows how much Thapelo blames himself for his mother's solitude. She is alone because his father could not abide a gay son. She was attacked because she is alone.

She lives in an RDP house the size of a matchbox. Not what Greg was expecting and a different world from Thapelo's Italianate townhouse, from his confident jokes and his love of mimosas at brunch. 'I wish we could have met under better circumstances,' Greg says and she takes both of his hands in hers.

'Never mind that,' she says, 'I'm just happy to finally meet you. Thanks for looking after my boy.' Her hands are cold and clammy. Her smile scrunches the skin around her eyes and makes the one eye look small and kind, curved downwards slightly towards her cheek. The other eye is swollen shut.

'He looks after me,' Greg says. He winks at Thapelo but Thapelo is watching his mother.

'Can I make you something to eat, Mama?'

'I'm not hungry,' she says. Then, 'Maybe a sandwich.'

In the kitchen, Greg arranges slices of white bread on three white plates. Thapelo cuts thick, uneven pieces of cheese. He sticks the end of his knife into the sealed plastic tray of ham that they brought with them from Woolies and the air makes a gunshot noise as it escapes. The flowers they brought are here, too, in a simple vase with orange and brown petals painted on it.

'You know, she's never met any of my boyfriends,' Thapelo says. He's composed himself after the initial shock of seeing her, although his eyes are still a little red.

'I think I'm a hit,' Greg says, flicking his hand from his face in the most diva-like gesture he can manage. He hopes the lightness helps. He hopes Thapelo knows he's not trying to minimise what's happening or make it about him. Thapelo sniffs and wipes his nose. He smiles as he butters the bread.

That night, the two of them lie very still in a room barely dark enough to sleep. Headlights move across the lace curtains. A dog barks somewhere in the distance. 'You okay in there, Ma?' Thapelo calls.

'I'm fine!'

Greg rolls away from the window. A minute passes. Another excruciating minute. Then the bed creaks and Thapelo's arm comes sliding under Greg's pillow. His other arm wraps around Greg's torso and pulls him in close. They sleep like that until morning.

You Can't Stay Here

Malusi touches the hot cloth to his cheekbone and winces. The split skin near his eye has scabbed over from last night, but he can't afford an infection. He needs to clean the wound, even if it means reopening it. He presses the wet heat into his face, wipes the dried blood away, repeats. The fucking men in this country. What the fuck is wrong with them?

He managed to get Nozipho's boyfriend off her before the bastard could rape her, but already she'd been hurt. Her lip was bleeding when Malusi broke down the door of her shack. She was on the bed, crying, and her boyfriend had his cock out and a quart of beer in his left hand.

'What do you want?' the boyfriend said. 'You want a turn?'

'Leave her alone,' Malusi said, his voice as deep as he could make it, his muscles tight with rage.

'Is this your other boyfriend?' the man said. He slapped Nozipho's face with his free hand, laughed.

Now Malusi might lose his job. The restaurant manager won't want a waiter with a bruised, swollen eye. It'll put the diners off their food, she'll say. He can just imagine the way she'll say it, too, that haughty disgust. He'll try to tell her he was protecting his neighbour, but she won't care. She doesn't like to hear about the drama of the townships. She acts as if hearing about it is the same as living through it. She just can't do it. I don't need to know about your private life, Malusi, she'll say, but looking like this at work is totally unacceptable. Maybe he can ask to swap with Samson for a few days, one of the Zimbabwean guys who cleans the dishes. Samson is handsome and polite, like all Zimbabweans. The diners would love him.

Malusi lights the flame on his butane cooker again and heats the soapy water some more. It must be hot hot to kill any bacteria. He wipes until the scab has dissolved. The cut is small. Maybe his boss wouldn't even notice it if it weren't for the swelling.

He wrings out the excess water from the cloth, wipes it over his armpits, his groin. He applies deodorant and puts on his cleanest shirt – white and crisp and respectable. There's a strange humming noise outside, like cheering, like the crowds at a soccer match at Green Point Stadium, although it obviously isn't that because Green Point is so far on the other side of the city it may as well be in another province. Is he hearing things because his head was hit? Humming. Buzzing. Ears can malfunction like that.

Trucks are parked along the main road at the newest edge of the settlement. Six of them, and more of them pull up as Malusi gets there. Soldiers leap out of them – bullet-proof vests, shields, guns – except they aren't real soldiers, most of them are simply people from other parts of the city just like this, hired to clear this part out. 'This is private land,' one of the bosses says on his loudspeaker. 'You can't stay here.'

This can't be happening again. Not again. He has only just managed to pay off the materials for his place last week. 'What's going on?' Malusi says to a teenage boy beside him.

'No, they're tearing down our shacks.'

Malusi checks his phone. He needs to be at work in an hour and it takes an hour to get there – three taxis, a ten-minute walk to the restaurant in the Waterfront – but his shack is only a few rows deep in that direction, the direction where the thugs are pouring into the township. It isn't long before the screaming starts, or had it been going all morning? A woman gets dragged out of her shack right in front of him. It's Phumla and she's holding her baby and trying to pull her sweatshirt closed but the soldier pushes her out of the way and signals to one of the drivers.

'You can't stay here,' the soldier says, 'this is illegal.'

Phumla yells at him. She isn't intimidated by his baton, by his gear. She's been through this all before, they all have. She gesticulates with her free arm – with the other, she bounces the baby on her hip. The driver revs the engine of his truck a few times as a warning. He hoots, and people scatter. Phumla tries to stand her ground and stare down the truck, but it accelerates towards her so fast it looks as if the driver won't stop – he wouldn't, would he? – and her resolve falters. She ducks out of the way just in time. Her baby starts to scream. She lifts the child into her arms and rocks it. The small face is wild, distraught, tears glisten on its cheeks. The truck rams into her shack. A crunching sound, but little resistance, as the wooden beams of the frame snap and the sheet metal collapses.

Malusi dials Nathi's number but the call won't connect. He's out of airtime. He sends a *please call me* and waits. No response. Nathi works for that non-profit that helps them when they get evicted. They had a court case about this a few months ago and it was supposed to have stopped these demolitions. Malusi was there. He attended in the public gallery of the court in the centre of town. It was a victory, they said. Their homes were safe. Their shacks couldn't be demolished without a court order, without being given somewhere else to live.

The truck reverses back over the remains of Phumla's shack and the debris subsides under its weight. Sheets of corrugated metal slide off to reveal the corner of a mattress. Malusi runs towards the commotion. Neighbours are scattering into their shacks, trying to pack their possessions as fast as they can, pulling out duvets and coffee cups and butane cookers and leaving them in the dirt on the far side of the road, in the uninhabited lot. Malusi tries to salvage something from Phumla's shack. Her baby's clothes, maybe, or some pans. He lifts a sheet of corrugated iron. The soldier pushes him out of the way.

'We're confiscating this stuff,' the soldier says, 'these structures are illegal.'

'I just want to see what's underneath.'

The soldier rams his baton right into the wound near Malusi's eye. The pain sears the world white and he stumbles, falls backwards onto his coccyx. From the ground he watches the soldiers swarm the shack like flies on a carcass. They carry off every one of the metal sheets and the shards of broken wooden frame and dump them all into a trailer that they've hired for the day. Already, the driver of the truck has changed direction, aimed the vehicle at another home.

The buzzing grows louder. An angry nest of wasps. Vuvuzelas in his ears. Malusi blinks hard to dispel the noise. It must be coming from inside his head – what else could it be? His phone rings. Nathi. 'Tell them what they're doing is illegal,' he says. 'Tell them they can't evict you without a court order.'

'Okay,' Malusi says, 'I'll tell them.'

'Ask to see the court order. They won't have one. I'll be there as quickly as I can.'

Malusi tries to find a sympathetic face among the men in riot gear. A black guy, very thin, so thin he must be hungry. He tells him what Nathi said. The soldier laughs. 'That's bullshit,' he says. It isn't bullshit, he remembers dancing on the steps of the court. He remembers hearing the judge's words, and reading them again in the papers the next day. It isn't bullshit; it's the law. But what help is the law?

By the time Nathi arrives, the soldiers have almost reached Malusi's home. They have torn down two of his neighbours' homes already, and they are busy with a third. Tearing at it with their hands, their batons, their vehicles. It looks like a scene from a war, and this war has flattened a residential area the size of three soccer fields. Soccer fields. Is this why he's been hearing stadium sounds all morning? The noise, that discordant roar, is growing louder all the time. He thought it was in his head but it can't be, surely his ears can't produce a sound like this. He thought it was cheering or buzzing but maybe what it is, now that it's so loud he can hear all the parts that make it up, is an accumulation of screams and sobs and scraping metal and breaking wood and fury and begging and grief. It's so loud Malusi can't hear Nathi when Nathi finds him. Nathi is saying something, he can see his lips move, but Malusi can't understand him. Please, he says, say that again.

Nathi has brought a lawyer with him, the beautiful law-yer who works with him at the non-profit, Refilwe, Malusi thinks, and lifts a hand to wave to her and she nods at him but she's busy filming the destruction. She pans her phone over the newly homeless, the soldiers, the trucks and dust. She approaches one of the men in riot gear and holds her phone up to his face and an altercation breaks out. Malusi can't hear their words but it's obvious the soldier feels pro-voked. He yells at Refilwe and tries to take her phone. She steps back, runs behind one of the shacks. Please God let her be uploading that video to Twitter. Let the journalists see it. Let there be someone who cares.

Tyres are burning on the main road now. Residents, too scared to confront the demolition team, dance and sing. Black smoke rises from the burning rubber, the petrol. It catches in Malusi's throat. The shack beside Nozipho's comes down. He hasn't seen Nozipho all morning. He runs back through the chaos and rams against the door of her shack. It gives way without much resistance, the lock still broken from last night. She is alone, asleep on her bed, face down.

'Nozipho!' he calls. 'Sisi!'

An explosion of cold deep in his chest. It ripples through his body. Is she . . .?

He takes hold of her head, carefully as he would a newborn baby's. It's cold, but not as cold as it would be if she were . . . He turns her face towards him. He places his index finger along her upper lip. There is breath. A shallow, warm breath.

'Hey,' he calls out of the door of her shack. 'Hey, someone's in here!'

But the soldiers don't react. He's invisible to them, impossible to hear. He's not a human any more but a symbol, a problem to be eradicated. People can't just squat wherever they like. There are rules. This isn't anarchy. The soldiers pillage the neighbouring shack. They steal the walls, the beams, the roof and put it all in their trucks. They are no longer human, either. They can't be reached. Malusi can't stop them. Not with words or the expression in his eyes or anything he does. Is it their capacity for reason that has failed, or their hearts? He returns to Nozipho, tries to gather her up with gentle movements. He wraps his left arm under her neck, his right arm beneath her knees and lifts, slowly, carefully. He's losing time, the truck might strike at any moment and kill them both on impact but she's concussed, she must be, or why is she still so oblivious to all this commotion going on around her? Nobody could sleep through this. Her boyfriend must have hit her harder than Malusi realised. He must have rattled her head, and you can't shake a concussed person. You can't run with them in your arms. The jolts will be too much for their swollen, bruised, delicate brain. He glides out of the shack, slow and smooth, his legs burning from the effort. He lays Nozipho down in the dirt on the far side of the road. He positions her on her back where there are no structures, where these monsters have no reason to return. He removes his shirt, his crisp white shirt that was meant to impress his boss who doesn't want to know about any of this, and he squashes it into a makeshift pillow. He pushes the ball of cloth beneath Nozipho's head.

When he looks up, two of the soldiers are laughing at an old woman being chased from her shack. Like Malusi, she has no shirt on. Her breasts are bare above her skirt and she tries to cover them up but the soldier chasing and shooing her walks too quickly and she keeps losing her footing and stumbling.

Malusi is running before he can think.

He runs towards the soldiers and he lowers his torso, his head, as he runs. He's going to tackle one of them with all of his strength, all of the rage in his blood. He's going to ram into this bastard's stomach so hard that it kills him, if it must, but the soldier sees him and ducks out of the way. Malusi's legs come to a halt but the rage does not stop. It has set fire to his insides. It feeds off the burning sun, the dancing flames of the burning tyres, the thick, black, poisonous smoke. It must find an outlet, a target.

A soldier waves to the driver of the truck. He directs the driver to Nozipho's shack.

Malusi runs into a group of neighbourhood children, crying, mostly, forgotten by their parents, and he pulls out a small boy. The child is about four years old, wide-eyed and silent, in a faded blue jersey. Malusi yanks him by the arm, just as the soldiers do, and he hears his mother scream as she runs after him but he is too quick. He lifts the boy and pushes him onto the roof of Nozipho's shack. The soldiers will not kill a boy. Even these heartless bastards wouldn't do that. Malusi pulls himself onto the roof to join the boy – an impossible feat, surely, but he has the strength of ten men, ten versions of himself who did nothing for too long, who stood and watched.

The roof is unsteady. The shack wobbles beneath their weight. Malusi finds his footing. He braces himself, feet wide above the corner beams, and he lifts the boy onto his shoulders. The child grips Malusi's head, sharp fingernails pressing into his flesh. The screaming, buzzing, roaring sound is so loud now that Malusi almost hopes that the little boy will press his tiny fingers into the wound near his eye. Anything to make this noise stop. Malusi grips the boy's foot against his chest with one hand and raises the other hand in a fist. They will not take anything more from Nozipho, from Phumla, from him. Someone is screaming at Malusi's feet, but the screams are lost in the cacophony. It's probably the boy's mother. She'll forgive him, she must know this is worth it. These bastards can't keep going, now. They can't destroy all of their homes. They have to stop for a child.

He can see forever from up here. In the distance, grey mountains push into the low, white cloud. There's a mosque about five kilometres to the west, small green minarets above the sea of shacks. An abandoned power station, train lines, a few distant housing projects and the freeway. Slums cover everything in between. Shacks and clothing lines and misery, pressed tightly together, spilling over each other and onto the verges. Nearby, the burning tyres, the new destruction, glistening white sand. Refilwe is being forced into the back of a police van. She looks up, nods at Nozipho. Nozipho watches Malusi. She's standing now, fully healed from her altercation last night. There are no bruises on her face, no swollen lip. How can she have recovered? She's shouting at him but he can't hear her. Is that his mother in the crowd? He could swear it's his mother, the day before she disappeared. It's the same skirt, the same doek as he remembers but it's clean now, no bloodstains, and she hasn't aged a day in all these years. She smiles at him and starts to shout but he can't hear her, he can't hear anything any more, it's total silence, and when did the light become so strange, so cool and white like moonlight reflected on still, black water?

His sister's also calling to him from between the soldiers, or is it his grandmother? They looked so similar – you could tell from the old photographs of his gran when she was young. She's pulling her cardigan closed and watching the police take her husband away, she's screaming at him but he can't make out her voice. He strains to hear what she's saying. There is no sound. He tries to focus on her lips, to read her lips, but there are thousands of people he hadn't noticed before, standing in the gaps between the soldiers and the residents he knows, the ones filming the eviction on their phones. These new people – where did they come from? – have no phones. They are dressed like people from the nineteen-forties and -fifties, the twenties, the eighteen hundreds. There are homeless people in rags and judges in great black robes. There are soldiers from the Frontier Wars, he's sure of it, he recognises the shields and the spears from illustrations he saw at school. They are watching him. They are shouting at him. They all face him, thousands and thousands of them, stretching over the dunes all the way to the mountain, an army waiting for his response, but what are they saying? They're shouting and gesticulating at him, they are getting agitated and he knows it's important, he knows he needs to hear them before it's too late.

He looks down. The soldiers in black clothes and bullet-proof vests are pulling at the sheet metal beneath him. One wall collapses, then the beam holding the roof gives in. The child on Malusi's shoulders is suddenly weightless. He himself is weightless, suspended in the air for an eternal second, but his body is falling. He calls out to the ancestors one last time, what do you want from me? But the words don't come out. His voice is trapped in the body that falls, the body that will be buried and forgotten, and the moon-white light is fading and Nozipho doesn't stop screaming at him, his mother doesn't stop screaming at him but the whole world is quiet as the womb. His skin glitters like the stars in the Eastern Cape night back when he was born, but the black smoke ripples towards him. It's everywhere now, not just in the burning tyres, and he can't read his mother's lips because she is nothing but smoke, a shadow between the shacks, and he, too, is nothing but shadows.

The Chair

A tiny green shoot emerges from the damp soil. Its green is fluorescent, bright as spring, a defiant magic of sunlight given form against the darkness of the forest. This is an enormous forest, larger than nations, but nations are yet to harden on maps. For now: witches and sprites, shadows and fire. The forest has been here since the glaciers retreated, absorbing generation after generation of men, women and children moving north. Were they fleeing the spreading deserts, the heat? History does not recall their reasons.

Plague enters the forest on the backs of rats. It clears out the nearby villages and towns. Bodies burning, buried, some left to rot in the open air. A little girl hides behind this sapling for a while and prays. It is the end of the world. What will become of her?

It is not the end of the forest. Not yet.

The sapling thickens. Breathes in the summers, stretches to the sky.

It drops its own acorns. It houses squirrels and hawks, snails, ten thousand creatures too small to notice. Tall as the sky, strong as a pillar of rock. French oak, they call it now.

Man lays claim to its life. Undeterred by nations, by systems of ownership, its leaves brighten, darken, fall, season after season after season. The planet spins. It orbits the sun.

They fell the tree at four hundred years old. Now, there's a supermarket parking lot where her trunk once stood. A checkout counter lined with glossy magazines, chocolate bars, and gum.

*

The wood is julienned, lathed into spindles and legs like candelabras. Steamed, bent. The pieces come together. Mortise and tenon joints. Carved, smooth saddle seat.

The chair is golden when finished. Silk to the touch.

A woman finds it in a shop on the high street of a small, dusty town at the colonial frontier in Africa, half a world away from the forest. She's middle-aged by then – light pools in the corners of her pale blue eyes – but the chair reminds her of her childhood across the oceans, in that cold, damp city where sewerage ran in the streets and the air was choked with soot and the rich turned up their noses at people like her. There was rain in those days. There was greenery. Relief from this endless drought, this merciless heat. The men knew craftsmanship and manners, unlike her brute of a husband. There was space for finery.

Is this a Windsor chair? she says. The style, I mean.

Yes, madam. Part of a dining set. Six chairs and this table.

Could I pay it off in instalments?

She passes the dining set to her daughter on her daughter's wedding day. Her daughter, who doesn't want this farm life in this barren valley where the sun bleaches the sky white and the land strains to produce anything that can be sold – chicory, cattle – where today the farmers have given up these ambitions and returned the earth to its wildness. Wildness can be sold, now, an escape from human meddling. Nature reserves and luxury camps, thatched and air-conditioned, a wild expanse stretching from horizon to horizon (but no further). Sightings of zebra and cheetah and giraffe. She can't see this. She knows only the valley of her childhood, of her time: the failed crops, the wars. The natives eye her with open hostility or, worse, despair, because this land is stolen, surely, it wasn't ours to take. She marries the wrong kind of settler, the kind who arrived before the British and lost the ways of Europe, but he's good to her. He listens. His eyes soften whenever she speaks and that's all that matters in the end, Daddy, surely that's enough to make you like him?

She takes the chairs with her when she moves. A city is rising on that deep vein of gold that runs through the earth and cities need all kinds of things besides chicory. The husband sells musical instruments to the saloons and she-beens. Grand pianos for the gold barons. But another war breaks out. The great red empire spills north. The sun never sets. The husband is killed for speaking the wrong language.

She is alone in the world now, a baby growing inside her. Just enough money to start a boarding house.

She makes cottage pie for the lodgers. Beef-and-onion stew. Roast beef on Sundays. There are fresh arrivals in the city every week. Boarding houses are full. She has miners and newspapermen, a tailor, two teachers. She places one of her oak Windsor chairs in each of the bedrooms. In 2B, the room next to the stairs, the first lodger sits in this chair to write letters to a woman he knew in his childhood. She never writes back. The next man to rent the room sits in this chair to sober up. Upright, the room doesn't spin the way it does when he lies on the bed. He stares out of the window at the bougainvillea growing wild in the sanitary lane behind the boarding house. He tries to count the bright pink flowers. Concentration helps him keep the tears at bay.

They age and die. The boarding house closes. The baby, full-grown now, inherits the chairs. She reunites the set – more ash these days than honey-coloured, cracked a little from lack of care. She oils them down, places them in a duck egg blue dining room with white wainscoting beneath un-smiling black-and-white portraits of her ancestors. They have dinner in these chairs for many years. Husband, wife, three children. Long silences; excellent posture. She rings the bell for the servants when their meal is done.

She is in this chair when she opens the letter. Her son has been shot down somewhere over North Africa. A Common-wealth victory, the vanquishing of the Fascists, but it haunts her in her old age. What was it all for, she mutters, we didn't win. We think we won but we became the enemy. Look around you, she says, but her daughters only smile and pat her gently on the hand. She doesn't ring for the servants any more. She doesn't give them English names. She asks them to stay and talk. Please, she says, sit. Tell me about your children.

She stares into the garden at sunset. She watches her long-dead son come striding up between the azaleas to join her for dinner. He pulls out the chair for her to sit, a proper gentleman. She raised him well. His strong hands on the smooth, warm oak. Don't go, she says when he finishes his coffee. I have a terrible feeling you won't come back. He winks at her and blows her a kiss. He never stops coming back.

The surviving children inherit a chair each. There are only two left from the set. No one knows where the others went. Lost in the unravelling of their mother's mind. Maybe she gave them to her carer, her daughter says. She loves the chair, even though it's terribly old-fashioned and doesn't go with any of her things. She likes modern and clean. No fuss. But this chair reminds her of her mother. She places it in the nook between the living room and the dining room, tucked under a small oak table with the telephone on top. A dial that clicks as it rotates. Replaced, in time, by square, bevelled buttons. Good evening, ma'am, may I please speak with Charlie?

She runs her hand over the thick, coffee-ringed yellow pages. It is polite, young man, to introduce yourself, she says, before rising to find her son.

When Charlie grows up, he has secret meetings. A hidden door to a windowless basement. Dark skin on that ancient wood. Dark skin where it isn't allowed to be. Sweat runs down their backs and soaks into the grain of the wood. They wait in the darkness, still and quiet, as police tramp through the house upstairs. Truncheons and handcuffs and threats. They can wait. A new country is coming. A candle too close to the chair sets the crest rail on fire. It chars at the end like a stick of incense, a petrol-bomb rag.

It's a revolutionary burn, Charlie says when he gives the chair to his son. You wouldn't believe who used to come to our safe house. Who was sitting in this chair when it got that burn.

I know, Dad, the son says, rolling his eyes. He's heard the story a hundred times.

The son needs it for his university digs. A rambling, creaking old house near campus, dwarfed by oak trees in the emerald green shadow of the mountain. European oak. There's an engineering student in the house, two architects and a theatre major, the only girl. Their house parties are legendary. At a come-as-your-favourite-historical-figure party, the chair loses a spindle, cracks another. Cleopatra glides into the living room, buzzed from a small line of coke she did in the bathroom, and sees Napoleon sitting in the chair

188

smoking a joint, talking to Freddie Mercury about the coming financial crisis. The banks are failing. Thousands of home foreclosures. It could be ten years before the economy recovers. Cleopatra lifts her slender, spandexed leg over Napoleon's lap and kisses him in the middle of his point about emerging markets. They fall backwards onto the floor laughing, kissing, the crash completely soundless against the voices in the room, the laughter, Rihanna playing so loudly on the portable speaker on the bookshelf that the police get called in to tell them to keep it down.

The chair sits in storage for a while after that. Cleopatra doesn't love it. Napoleon agrees it's a little tired. Charred at the top, ashy, webbed with hairline cracks and two broken spindles. He doesn't want to give it away but they shouldn't be hoarding. A baby is coming – and they'll have so much clutter for that. Prams and mobiles and bassinets.

The woman who buys the chair pays fifty rand cash to take it off his hands. An internet deal. She arranges her own transport.

It's strapped down now in the back of a metallic blue Toyota Hilux, hurtling along the freeway on a hot, windy February afternoon. The woman sits in the passenger seat up front. She can't drive and it isn't her bakkie, but a friend agreed to help her. She doesn't know the history of the chair, she doesn't know the style, but it's beautiful. It'll be the most beautiful thing in her home, the small space she shares with her girlfriend who no one knows is her girlfriend.

It's handmade, you can see, not plastic and mass-produced in China.

They drive past the abandoned power station to the left, past the signs to the airport, to Nyanga. They take the off-ramp and enter the dry, sandy township, so far from any forest, from any oak trees. She imagines having a child of her own one day, a little girl who'll grow up with something beautiful like this in her home. The spindles look like the candlesticks she's seen in the window of that fancy interiors shop on Kloof Street. The chair's like something out of a fairy tale castle. A chair fit for a princess. She doesn't mind the cracks, the burn, the breaks. The wood's a golden honey colour beneath the scuffs, you can see. A little sandpaper and varnish – it'll be good as new.

Acknowledgements

Some of the stories in this collection are brand new. Earlier versions of the others have been published before: 'The Lucky Ones' was first published in *Brittle Paper* in 2020. 'Young People Problems' was published in *Adda,* the online literary magazine of the Commonwealth Foundation, in 2020.

I have been lucky enough to have three stories published in *New Contrast:* 'Quiet as Ants' in 2018, 'Fever Tree' in 2019, and 'The Chair' in 2022.

'The King of the Jungle' was originally published online in *Penny,* which was then turned into an illustrated, miniature paperback called *The Other,* published in the USA in 2017.

'Going Home' first appeared in the anthology *Queer Africa II: New Stories,* published in South Africa in 2017. It was then chosen for the anthology *Queer Africa: Selected Stories,* published in the UK in 2018.

'Why Don't South Africans Read Fiction?' was first published in *The Kalahari Review* in 2018.

Thank you to the editors of the literary magazines and anthologies and websites that published me along the way - you really helped to buoy my spirits and keep me writing. Special thanks to Makhosazana Xaba and Karen Martin who were the first to publish a story I wrote.

'Always in Motion' was written in Stellenbosch in 2022, during a writing retreat hosted by FicSci, a project of the NRF SARChI in Science Communication. Thank you to Prof. Malebogo Ngoepe, whose research inspired this story, and to Prof Mehita Iqani and Dr. Wamuwi Mbao for creating and running the retreat, and for editing the anthology that came from it, *flow: FicSci 01*, published by African Minds in 2023.

The podcast that Beth listens to in 'Little Grey Blazers' is a *Modern Love* episode, originally an essay for the *Modern Love* column, 'From He to She in First Grade', written by Laurie Frankel, and published in *The New York Times* in 2016.

The book referenced in 'Kingdom of Prophets' is *Landmarks*, by Robert Macfarlane, published in 2015. It was my introduction to literary nature writing, and the permission I needed to wax lyrical about fynbos and Afromontane forests the way that I do. If you're interested in the relationship between language and the natural world, I can't recommend it enough.

Thank you, as always, to my publisher Stevlyn Vermeulen and to the team at Kwela. Thank you Danya Ristić-Schacherl for your thoughtful edit of the manuscript. Thank you to my friends and family, for your unwavering love and support. Thank you to my readers, for choosing to spend your time with me. My mother, Brigid, always insisting on reading any story I've written as soon as I'm willing to share it and, once published, joyously spamming everyone with the link. Thank you for your fierce belief in me. And Michael, my first reader, best friend, partner in life and love, thank you for everything.